TCO

First Edition, 2023

TCO

Graeme Bennett

Published by Graeme Bennett Ltd.

CONTENTS

CONTENTS

Down the Rabbit Hole

June 2009

It was just after 4:30 on a warm and sunny June afternoon in the London borough of Hackney district known as Hoxton. There, on a shady sidewalk at the edge of a green space called Hoxton Square, a handbill distributor dressed in jeans, sneakers, and a light-grey hoodie emblazoned with a Moloko logo was chatting up passers-by. He'd approach the ones who looked to be young and hip and, if things went well, they'd be handed a hot-off-the-press, full-colour, graffiti-inspired handout that he'd proudly tell them was his own creation. "Hi," he'd say. "My name's Len. Are you from around here?"

Len was well positioned to intercept stragglers coming down from New City College on the north side and the local workers, some of which always somehow managed to end their days at 4:30 p.m. "There are usually a few unicyclers and wildly arty types that head this way from the Circus school, too," he was explaining to the girls who stayed to listen to his patter. "It's just over that way about a hundred paces or so," he said with a west-directed nod. "You know the place—the old electric station? It's a big red thing..." he added with a wink.

"Oh, you wish," grinned the mark.

Len moved back to the pitch. "Everything in the London art scene converges here, y' see?" he enthused. "These are *our* people, our *audience*. The 18-to-28 crowd. The alive ones. Like you lovely ladies. So, you gonna come to this thing tonight?"

The girls smiled and shrugged. The mark wrinkled her nose a little.

"You don' wanna miss this one, luvs. It'll be a real banger. Live music, crazy art pieces—and I mean really crazy, fantastic stuff." He shouted after them as they shrugged and headed off. "It's gonna be brilliant!" A nearby pedestrian looked at him with mild alarm. He held out a handbill like a peace offering. "Sorry, Miss. Didn't mean to shout. Party at a big art event tonight. Interested?" She shook her head and hurried past him without a word.

He could weed out the corpos and the tourists immediately. Some of them were headed southwest to the buses on Old Street; others were trekking to the overground station northeast of here. This time of year, many of the art school types had their final project portfolios with them, so they were instantly identifiable as they crossed the square.

He did get hassled for soliciting now and then. But that was rare and he had never been issued a ticket. He'd never even seen a police officer on foot in this area. They would just drive by from time to time, barking mostly incomprehensible warnings over their loudspeaker.

You there. Mooffleon! Yanadalod tabedehr!

They were too fat and lazy to get out for anything but a serious crime. On the rare occasion he might not notice them approaching, the coppers would just tell him to move along and, if they did, he'd just cross the square and continue on the other side. No problem. But the east side was by far the best for street traffic, and this shady spot near the black iron fence gate was his preferred position.

Len was introducing himself as 'Lucky Len' to his latest mark and explaining how he had come to be a regular fixture at this spot. In fact, his story was considerably more elaborate than the truth. In actuality, he'd simply moved around the corner to this location from his old haunt on the south side of the square, in front of the glass-topped building that formerly housed the White Cube art gallery in Hoxton. It was iconic, but it was also empty and available for rent, on what had become a decidedly dead side of the square.

But Len was telling a tale as lively as the park was today. "Moving out of that old dump, y'see, had been the biggest change since I'd left Bristol 'bout five years ago. Yeah, five and a bit actually. I was new to London, of course, and hadn't realised what a naff neighborhood I was getting into. So bad. And trapped in a two-year lease! I know, it was terrible. It was finally up, and I was able to move out of the old trash heap and step up a bit, y'know? Found a new flat, yeah. Funny thing was, I was pissed about the whole moving thing at the time. I'd finally got a job at the print shop and started to get a decent crew of mates and poof, it all went up in smoke, y'know? But now I've got a proper studio set up. Yeah, I make all these cards and posters and things, like that one. So you gonna come tonight? Great, see you there then. Cheers."

Len never mentioned it, but his 'proper studio' was really just his bedroom. His desk was reasonably well equipped with a computer, printer and a suite of not-quite-up-to-date graphics software, but it was still just a bedroom. He still lived with his dad and mum just a few blocks from here, in an almost respectable brownstone tenement building up on Fanshaw. The new flat was at least in a neighborhood where he could chain his bike up outside for a few hours without having it nicked or pulled to bits. That was a welcome change from their old place by the tracks, where things were so bad that the city finally installed bike bunkers to cut down on the appalling levels of thievery. He was glad to leave that—and his old nickname—behind. He was no longer the slippery, wishy-washy one they called "Liquid Len." He was above that now. That was the thing about Hackney—well, all of London, really. The neighborhoods had such distinct character, they made *you* a different character. Hoxton and Shoreditch were the heart. The art at the centre of it all.

When Len's parents had first moved to Fanshaw, the

gallery on the square was already closed, so he had it in his mind that his location was due for a change. He'd tried out a few locations without much success. The area just south of the station seemed like it should have been perfect—lots of foot traffic, of course—but it just wasn't good. The closer you got to Hoxton Station, the more ethnic it got. Nothin' wrong with that but they generally weren't interested in his particular wicket. Fortunately, the hot young Indian girls were usually good for a chat—and they did love to dance. And there was that fine-as-wine black girl that lived in that neighborhood. It was a shame to leave her behind.

Len didn't think too much about moving out. Life at home was not all that bad, and he had enough money from this 'studio' business to have a little fun now and then. Maybe if he really got a steady relationship happening with someone....

Here on the east side of the square, the late afternoon crowd manifested in amusing ways. This time of day, there were usually a few old Pearly Queens heading home from church, always smiling. And this week, for some reason, there were quite a few upscale types in their Sloanie designer apparel and luxury handbags, wandering around. Probably took a wrong turn somewhere. Hopefully this was not another sign of the gentrification that was already out of control in the south end of Hoxton. The designer brand types were not his target audience.

He imagined himself explaining to the crowd how it worked.

"Well, you see, every time a couture designer brand outlet

shows up in this neighbourhood, a bell rings. And every time that bell rings, a street artist gets his or her wings—and they just fly away. Forever."

Fact of the matter was that Len didn't really understand the crowd that the Moloko club/event space/art show was targeting for this event. This was a decidedly upscale event, with an admission price and well-heeled clientele to match. And, as much as Len might disapprove, they came with their designer labels, Italian shoes, and the usual range of high-priced vices.

The good news was that they also bought art. Expensive art—the kind where you get to sit with the art in a well-lit private room to imagine how it will look when it's hanging on *your* wall. The kind a gallery account executive will take you out to a fancy restaurant to close a deal over.

Len was more of a street art *connoisseur*. Beautiful graffiti wall art, building-scale supergraphics, stencil art, and those sorts of things—those were the Shoreditch landmarks that identified it as Ground Zero of the London street art scene. And the people that made this art and loved this art—they were Len's people. Specifically, Len looked for any of the telltale signs of the arty types: well-worn vintage clothes or perhaps a themed T-shirt or hoodie. Arty girls were easy to spot.

Coloured hair, ponytail, beads, or a cool tattoo was always a good sign. A guy with a hipster beard used to be a good indicator but now...? The girl with the buttons all over her backpack and that guy carrying the guitar? For sure. The targets were generally in their twenties, although he didn't miss a chance to chat up attractive women well outside that range.

Most of the freaks and geeks in the Hoxton area knew Len,

at least by sight. He was often here in the afternoons, always with a pack full of hot-off-the-press handouts to give away. Len did the designs and colour seps himself and worked with a couple of local print shops to produce the final products. In less than three years, he had gone from a part-time designer of one-off showcards and single-colour offset handbills to a proper poster business with a sponsored advertising model that actually made money. Not enough to afford a car or anything too crazy, but enough to keep going, producing and handing out A5-size minis and those big, beautiful bluebacks.

In the early evenings, he was usually on the move with his pack full of rolled-up posters, and his can of spray-glue. The posters, printed on special water-resistant outdoor paper called blueback, would end up wherever the client needed them, usually in a 12-block radius around whichever club or gallery was paying the bill.

Moloko was invested enough to pay for proper poster paper and full colour. They sometimes went for silk-screened posters or simple two-colour jobs, but in this case, they paid for four-colour process on really nice blueback stock for the larger outdoor posters, and decent card stock for these handouts. Len had used fluorescent cyan, magenta and yellow inks so the colours really popped this time. "And these cards are good enough," thought Len, "that I might be able to persuade a few other clubs or galleries to pay the piddlin' extra amount it cost to run in day-glo colours like these." It was *so* worth it for a night like tonight.

Tonight, though, the required minimum of 50 posters had

already been put up. And there were just two dozen more handouts to distribute. Tonight was The Big Show.

"Hey guys, lookin' for something good this weekend? Big thing at the Moloko club, see?" He held out three handbills and had two takers. "You know the place, yeah?"

The tallest of a trio of art-school guys nodded. "Yeah, thanks." His friend, who was not quite as tall, studied it for a moment, shrugged and stuffed it in his pocket.

"All right, any time after 9 pm. Cheers," said Len as the trio walked away. "Cool, thanks."

"Let's 'ave a look," said the shortest one of the three as the tall one looked at the handbill and then flipped it over. It was blank on the backside. He handed it to shorty. "You can have it." He elbowed the other fellow. "It's a bit much, don'cha think?"

"What, the design?" said his buddy.

"No, you git. The price. A bit fucking much money."

Shorty was still studying the text on the other handbill. "150 quid at the door? Jeez, that's pricey, all right." He ran down the feature list: three bands, laser lights, neon art, and complimentary champagne. "Looks like it might be pretty good, though. Light show, live music, psychedelia-type stuff by the look of it. Quite an event."

"I s'pose," said tall guy. What's that they're callin' it—a "hallucidelia happening?""Whatever *the fock* that is," said the middle one.

"It's a 'lucid dream,' says here. *Lu-cid in the sky...*" he sang.

"It's a pretentious load of bollocks, you mean."

"You've just not ingested the right amount of illicit substances, that's all that means."

"Not yet, mate, not yet."

Middle guy pulled a £20 note from his pocket. "This note's got 'pub fund' written on it. *My* pub fund."

"Well I might go, later, y' know?" said shorty.

"But you're coming to pub with us?"

"Y'of course!" He folded the handbill and attempted to insert it into his back pocket. But it flew away in the breeze. "Aw, bugger." By now it was a dozen paces away.

"Oh fock that," said the middle one, looking at his watch. "C'mon, we don't wanna be late for that meeting…"

"Hey, look," said tall guy, looking at his phone as they walked away. "Change in plans. Look at this…."

A few seconds later, the fluttering handbill ended up under the foot of a young man with a wispy beard and a backpack with a Canadian flag logo on it. He picked it up, unfolded it and showed it to the young woman accompanying him. A few metres away, Len watched them with interest as the two of them stopped in their tracks to examine the handbill. She looked at the artwork his design appreciatively. "Very nice. Kind of an *Alphonse Mucha* thing going on there," she said in a mild French-Canadian accent.

"Ooh, I like the way you pronounce that," Len heard her companion say. "Mu *sha*. I always thought it was pronounced 'Mookka'," the young man observed.

Len had learned what he had been told was the correct pronunciation of the name, the way it was spoken in the artist's native Czech dialect, pronounced as *Muh-ha*, but he didn't intervene, as he had heard other French people pronounce it this way, too. She was right on the money about the *art nouveau* design inspiration, though.

"In Quebec, and I think in Paris, too, we say Mu *sha, mon cher*," she said. "But I think it might be pronounced differently in English."

"Well, it really sounds better your way, I must admit," conceded her companion.

She smiled wanly. He always wants to be agreeable.

'Should I say something?' wondered Len, but he thought better of it and kept his mouth shut. He couldn't help but feel that his eyes were flashing like a "Wrong way!" sign as he looked at her, though.

"Looks like it might be *kinda* cool," Len overheard her say as she read the smaller print.

Her companion gasped when he saw the price. "Whoa, 150 pounds at the door? That's too rich for my blood."

The pair started walking again and as they moved closer to Len, they noticed he had a handful of the handbills. The young woman passed the one in her hand back to him. "Nice design, she said. "It's too good to throw away." Len nodded appreciatively and held the handbills over his head. "Big event at the Moloko club tonight. Read all about it."

"Sorry, thanks anyway," her partner said, sounding very Canadian indeed.

It didn't matter much to Len. He only had about twenty more flyers to get rid of anyway. He straightened a dog-eared corner on the one that had been returned and handed it off to a closest one of a pair of tidy looking young men. "One for your friend?"

"One what?" The other replied and the men both laughed at their naughty innuendo.

Len was counting them down now. One went into the hand of a well-dressed man, and the woman accompanying him took one, too. Another went into the purse of a young woman dressed like a nurse. Another three went to a trio of gum-chewing girls and other one to a woman wearing a rather fashionable hat.

It occurred to Len that, at first glance, some of the takers might have thought the figure of this art nouveau-inspired beauty was advertising some sort of fashion show. Which, in a way, it was. He'd drawn his inspiration from classic 1960s rock concert posters—and those were indeed inspired by the art nouveau style of artists such as Alphonse Mucha.

Finally he was down to one. It went into the tanned hands of an attractive blonde French girl. She pulled a pen out of her purse and used the back of the flyer to write down her phone number and then handed the flyer to the well-dressed and impeccably coiffed young man accompanying her.

The young man folded it and put it into his shirt pocket. "My name's Alec," he said to her. "I'll text you the address. I'll take care of everything."

She watched as the dark-haired young man and his expensive haircut headed off in the same direction as Len, toward the train station.

Len's next stop was somewhere for a quick bite to eat. As he stood at the Sandwich Express counter, he watched the dark-haired fellow just outside the window, typing on a mobile phone. Probably texting her, thought Len.

Alec was actually scheduling a meeting with his crew. In a few hours they'd be off to the club district in nearby Shoreditch.

He took the train from Hoxton station down to Shoreditch High Street. Emerging from the perennially dank smell of the overground station into the early evening light, Alec's senses were immediately reawakened by the familiar sights and smells of the area. The area always seemed to be in flux, with construction, or a new painting, or lorries rumbling up the A10 with a load of rubble from some new teardown. You'd barely step off the train and you'd already be able to see that this was the heart of the street art district. Every wall in sight was a piece of art. Alec loved the wall paintings between here and Chance Street—well, most of them, anyway—and he frequented many of the cafes and clubs in this part of town, from Sclater down through the Redchurch and Chance Street area.

The club was in that great area near Whitby Street and Chance. Alec felt a bit of pride that some of his earliest tags were still on the walls there. Unlike the claustrophobic spaces of better-known underground clubs like The Corollary and Nufo, Moloko was positively cavernous and fairly spectacular in its former warehouse digs. He was early enough tonight that he'd be sure to get in.

Alec pulled out the handbill and texted the map of the corner to the number Danielle had written on the back. When the text was sent, Alec flipped the handbill over gave it a closer look. Friday and Saturday only, it said, the Moloko club was hosting an all-night "hallucidelia" gallery and "psyche event" installation. The theme was "A Lucid Dream."

It was perfect.

Alec was well equipped for this, having brought a bagful of magic mushrooms and a couple of dozen tabs of synthemesc, hidden in a concealed inner pocket. He'd sell enough to cover his costs and the price of a few drinks. He wasn't sure he would be one of the first 100, but if so, there was complimentary champagne, too. Cheers to that!

Ten minutes later, Len arrived, his backpack now emptied of all commitments. As he scanned the line ahead of him, he recognised several of the people he'd talked to over the past few days. A couple of the art school guys were there and with them, this tall dark-haired fellow in a leather jacket. The three of them had been looking around and talking amongst themselves. As Len watched, the dark-haired fellow turned toward him and gave a two-finger salute of recognition. Len, assuming the guy must have recognised him, responded with a raised hand. But the stranger's head was tracking something else. Len followed the direction of his gaze and realised, with mild embarrassment, that the stranger apparently hadn't been signaling to him after all, but had instead been addressing a young blonde woman who was now approaching him. In fact, the stranger had indeed seen and recognised Len, but chose not to acknowledge his awareness of him. His attention remained laser-focused on the young woman's approach, which had the desired effect upon her.

She smiled as she took a position next to him ahead of Len in the line.

Len watched their interactions with some fascination at the non-verbal language in play. The dark-haired fellow moved in close to her ear, apparently speaking secretively to her. She responded with a flirtatious smile, quite aware there were other eyes watching. Len could understand why, of course, as he watched this young blonde woman draw attention. It was magnetic.

The dark-haired fellow wasn't concerned in the slightest about what anyone else in that line was doing. He was thinking of the lyric "hovering like a fly, waiting for the windshield on the freeway...."

Two

A Curious Hall

From his vantage point behind them, Len could readily see that the stranger had a certain charisma—an aura of cool confidence that women found attractive. Well, this one seemed to, certainly.

Len listened with mild amusement as the stranger introduced the others to her as "my crew" and presented her to them as "Danielle." Len gathered, by the snippets of conversations he could hear, that this fellow's name was Alec.

Alec toyed with her, this girl he'd met just a few hours earlier in the square. She made small talk and told him how she was in town to shop for a vintage jacket. He complimented her clothes and she told him she got them at the vintage shop down on Cheshire. "Fantastic place, great threads," she said.

"You think they'd have anything there for me, maybe?"

"Maybe," she shrugged. "You looking for a skirt or a dress?"

"Oh, I like a skirt."

"I can see that," she smiled.

"You're all right to get in, yeah?" Alec was almost 20 and he still almost always got carded at the door. They did tend to be a bit more lax with the pretty girls, though.

"Of course. See?" She held up an ID card.

"Looks legit. Is it?"

"I won't say," she smiled.

"Fantastic, we'll be in then."

The metal door creaked open and a doorman emerged with two posts and a length of braided rope. "Hey," she said, "I think the door's opening."

"Ooh, they've got the fancy rope out. Must be a *tres* posh affair."

As the doorman hooked the clasps on the ropes to the chrome-plated posts, the stragglers and loose ends at the back of the line suddenly snapped into place. A moment later, the line began inching forward as coats and IDs were checked and people were granted entrance into the event.

When he got to the door, Len said, "I'm on the guest list."

The doorman ran a fat finger down the list. Len was delighted to learn that his name was indeed on the guest list, as had been promised.

"Where's Bob Mack?" he asked the doorman as he got his hand stamped.

"Ask her," the burley fellow said, pointing to the coat check area.

"Hi, I'm Len, I did all the promo posters and, uh, these things," he said, pulling a dog-eared handbill from the side-pocket of his pack.

"Very cool, nice to meet ya," said the woman behind the counter. "By the way," she added, pointing to the pack, "You'll have to check that."

"Yeah, of course, no problem. Here y'go."

She handed him a ticket stub.

"Great, thanks." He peered into the semi-darkness of the corridor leading to the hall. "Say, d'you know if Bob Mack's around?"

"Yeah, he's here. I think he's up on the stage. D'ya know what he looks like?"

"Yeah, he knows me. I just wanna tell him about the posters, thanks."

In fact, Len also wanted to be paid for the work. Bob had been a client long enough that Len now only requested fifty percent of the bill in advance. That paid for the paper and the printing costs. Now, he would finally get his cut.

As his eyes adjusted to the dim lighting, Len got his first look at the event he'd been helping to promote all week. He walked past a row of huge scaffolds along the wall. On top of them were what looked like projectors and spotlights. A few spots appeared to be motion controlled, roving like searchlights across the floor, illuminating areas of the walls, stage and floor.

The first band was not yet on stage, but there was some light electronic dance music playing at a low volume over the PA system. A couple of roadies were working on the lights and cabling around what appeared to be a DJ podium. There was a drum kit, too. So this looked like it might not be a strictly EDM-only affair. The place was decked out more elaborately than Len had ever seen it. He spotted Alec and the blonde down by the stage.

A second set of huge scaffolds stood at the periphery of the stage area and between them hung a giant screen, where op-art animations were already playing. There, silhouetted by the dancing patterns, was the man Len was looking for. He was talking to a man with headphones around his neck. He looked over and saw Len as he approached.

"Hey Lennie," he said. Len hated being called that.

"Hi Bob. Hey, can I have a quick chat with you?"

"I'll be right with you," said Bob. He led the man with headphones over to the side of the stage and pointed to a breakout box. He patted the man on the back and disappeared into the darkness behind the stage. A few seconds later, a side door opened and he approached Len.

"How many of those handbills have we distributed so far?" asked Bob.

Len did a little arithmetic. "Seventy-five a day times four days, plus a hundred today is, uh, four hundred by my count. As promised."

"An' how about the posters?"

"Really good. I put up all fifty of the big ones. I got your posters in just about every record store, and all over the Shoreditch area. All the way to Stepney Green on the east side and the A1 on the west. And all around Islington College and the university."

"Good, good. Come on up to the office and I'll cut you a cheque."

"Great, thanks." The so-called gig economy hadn't been

particularly kind to Len when it came to the distribution part of his business. He'd worked—and paid for his own transportation and food—for roughly 7 hours a day all week. For a lousy half a quid per handbill. At least the posters paid a little better than that.

Len followed Bob up the stairs to the mezzanine and into his office. As he closed the door, Bob unlocked the desk drawer and pulled out a big chequebook. "Listen, ah, we've gotta talk about your distribution an' all that," he said as he watched Len's expression droop. "I've got a kid who'll do it for a lot less. And we're gonna get a printer and print 'em ourselves. So I dunno, maybe just give me a quote for distribution alone and we'll see...."

Len was stunned. Moloko had been one of his most reliable customers. And this was the third bailout this month.

"Gee Bob, that's really disappointing," said Len quietly. He tried to think of something else worth saying but couldn't.

"Ya I know—sorry mate." Bob scribbled a signature and put down the pen.

Len struggled to come up with reasons to reconsider as he watched Bob fold the cheque back and forth along its perforation line before detaching it from its stub. "You know you won't be able to print on that special poster paper, the blueback stuff...."

"Yeah, we'll prob'ly jus' use the cheap stuff, y' know? Times are tough, Lennie. But hey, thanks a lot, good job. Here ya go." He slid the cheque across the desk.

"Thanks," mumbled Len, as he folded the cheque and pocketed it.

Bob closed the chequebook and pushed it back into the top drawer. "You'll give me that distribution quote before next week?" he said as he locked the drawer. When he raised his eyes, the office door was being pulled shut.

* * *

Len stopped at the bottom of the mezzanine stairs, his heart racing. He was suddenly much less interested in partying. He considered his options. On the plus side was the fact that the arrangement with Bob had actually been a pretty sweet deal for him while it lasted. Bob paid for the materials and the printing, but there were always a few—and sometimes more than a few—extra posters to sell or give away. Better still was the fact that Bob and he had a "share and share alike" arrangement, where Bob could do what he wanted with his posters, but so could he. Either one of them could reprint them or use them as they saw fit. "So," Len told himself, "at least I still own my artwork. That's more than most commercial artists can say."

And there was the math that made his 'free' posters available. Bob wanted fifty big posters, so Len spec'ed them as A1 size—exactly half the size of the largest A0 paper his local offset press was able to handle. And Bob always wanted handbills. Those were spec'ed as A5 size. Len could get 400 of those by printing them "eight up" on each of the fifty pieces of A0 paper. That very conveniently left fifty pieces of A2 size 'blank' paper left over. Except the paper didn't need to be blank. It was being run through the same press and paper cutter as the other items, after all, and they were already paid for.

So Len would use the 'free' space to print his own projects, like business cards, art pieces, or, in this case, a limited edition "gallery size" edition of his new poster.

After this moment of reflection, his mood brightened and he stepped into the gathering crowd in the main event space.

On the stage, a DJ was live-mixing some extremely bass-heavy avant-garde music.

Behind the stage, a couple of musicians (Len doubted they would be famous enough to have roadies!) were tuning their guitars. Most of the people out on the floor were clustering around the Burning Man-esque art 'podiums' that dotted the floor of the cavernous warehouse-like artspace. The enormous figures—a pair of LED-illuminated wireframe hands here, an eyeball with neon-lit wings there, and a colour-shifting dragon over there—created a dream-like atmosphere that, Len had to admit, was as trippy as the event's posters had promised it would be.

This might be the high-water mark of the whole art scene, thought Len. Perhaps it will all be downhill from here. The investment bankers and luxury office developers will take over this neighborhood the way they'd already taken over Hoxton, and there will be no more enthralling dreams like these to delight and behold, save for the young and rich.

Len noticed a marked difference in the dress and manner of the attendees at a high-rent affair like this, versus the types who usually show up at a nightclub event. The ones here were the "pinky extended" types, sipping their complimentary glass of champagne and dressed in handsome ways befitting their affluent status. It stung a bit to realise that, despite his best efforts, these were indeed the designer label types, in large part. These were the types who thought of themselves as patrons, not nightclubbers. Len wasn't the least bit surprised to see that the big art pieces all had corresponding price tags affixed.

"Hey," said a voice behind him. It was Alec and the blonde. "Hi. The name's Alec. And this is Danielle."

It was Mr. Expensive Haircut. "Hi. I'm Len."

"Hey, I saw you talking to Bob Mack. You know him, eh?"

"Yeah, I designed the posters for this thing."

"Yeah, I know," said Alec.

"They're very nice," said Danielle playfully, her French accent showing.

"Hey, you wanna hang with us?" asked Alec. "I've got a few friends over there I'd like you to meet."

"Yeah sure," said Len.

As they crossed the floor, Danielle leaned in close to him

and said, "Hey, we've got some synthemesc. Do you want to take some with us?"

"Seems like the perfect place to do it," smiled Len as they walked past the huge dragon with the glowing eyes.

"This is Johnnie and Dal." Len recognised them—the short art school guy and his loutish friend. "You're the hand-bill guy, right?" said Johnnie.

"Ten points for Griffindor. You are correct, sir," replied Len.

"Oh yeah, that's you," said Dal. "Y'know, he lost yer fockin' poster thing. We couldn't even find this place until Alec told us where it was." He pointed a thumb at Johnnie. "And *he* had to borrow money to pay for his Tiki juice. But we made it."

He was either drunk or an idiot—and possibly both, Len realised. He made mnemonic mental notes, which he often used to remember names: Johnnie he would remember as John Knee-high and Dal he would remember as dull. "Hey, where's your tall friend?"

"Oh, you mean Paulie? He couldn't come tonight," said Johnnie. "'Cause he pissed away all his dosh at the pub," added Dal.

Len made another mental note: Paul equals tall. And never tell *anything* you want kept a secret to Dal.

"And this," said Alec, "This is Georgia. She owns the Smash Gallery. They did the neon stuff here."

Georgia nodded and smiled, her brown eyes sparkling behind long dark bangs.

Len looked up at the graceful neon wings flanking the eyeball. "Very nice. I always liked Rick Griffin."

Georgia smiled and drew in closer. "You know about him? Cool. Yeah, he had a great style. This is our tribute to that whole California sun-and-surf culture."

As the synthemesc kicked in, the music, the laser lights and the geometric patterns on the giant screen combined with an effect that was almost overwhelmingly hypnotic. Georgia lavished a great deal of her attention on Len and they danced and laughed and held hands like they'd known each other for years. Like old-school mescaline, a synthemesc trip lasted about 12 hours, so they were still riding on the high side when they finally tumbled out into the morning light just after 6 am the following morning.

Johnnie and Dal had wandered off a few hours earlier, it seemed. Alec and Danielle were nowhere to be seen.

"Hm. I'm glad I'm not driving," said Georgia. "I probably could, but driving while actively hallucinating is almost certainly a bad idea."

"...said anybody who knows anything at all about Hunter S. Thompson," added Len. "I hear you. I know I wouldn't want to be driving in this state of mind. Do you live close by?"

"Yeah, really close, in fact. Just up the A10. You know, High Street."

"Just over here then? Brilliant. Let's walk."

She pointed north. "I live up that way about six blocks. Near the bridge. In fact, sort of under the bridge. It's not that great a place, to be honest. But it's home. Will you walk with me?"

"That would be *splendid*. Are you warm enough?"

"Not really, but I'm fine."

He offered her his zip-up hoodie.

"Oh ho ho," she said as she zipped it up. "This is very snuggly. Much better."

"My house is in this exact direction, too, about eight blocks up," he said.

"No way. Really?"

"Yeah, I'm up by the post office on Hoxton Street—just past the art school."

"That's a bit more than eight blocks."

"Well, eight long blocks. Proper imperial size blocks. Only about a five-minute walk."

"We don't have to go that way. I'm just up ahead."

"I think I'll be drawing for a while when I get home," Len said. "My mind is absolutely brimming over with images. It's times like this when I like to have my sketchbook with me."

"I have a sketchbook, but I don't usually carry it with me," said Georgia. "I mostly do abstract doodles these days. Ha. What does that say about me?"

"Hey, nothing wrong with abstract doodles. Some of my best friends are abstract doodlers." He pointed northwest. "By the way, are we going in the right direction? I'm just walking here."

"Yeah, it's just about two more blocks. One west and one north."

"This is the street here," she said, pointing. "Just down at the end of the block on the right," she said as they approached her building.

"It feels strange for this to be ending," Len confessed. "That synthmesc is still in my brain. It must be for you, too?"

"Oh yes, definitely," she nodded.

"Will you be all right, tripping on your own?"

"Yeah, it's fine," she said. "I'm pretty tired. But thanks for walking with me." She unzipped the hoodie and handed it back to him. "That was a fun night."

"I really enjoyed meeting you. G'night." He leaned in for a possible kiss and got a hug. No worries.

A few minutes later he was at his own doorstep. The lights were all off, which was a relief. He didn't want to have to face mum and dad with dilated pupils. The keys and the lock seemed enormously noisy as he opened the door of the flat and closed it behind him. He slipped into his room and turned on the desk light. He still felt a little too wired to sleep, so he amused himself by doodling a few designs in his black book. He'd been trying to come up with an interesting graffiti idea to commemorate the city's rich sports history. (Hackney Marsh, after all, was said to have the largest single collection of football pitches in the world!)

Initially, he'd thought that the design should focus on football, but other elements kept inserting themselves into his imagination. Zing!—a dart scuttled by like a phosphorescent fish and hit a bullseye. A tennis racquet was swung. A basketball bounced. They all wanted to be part of the design, too, bouncing around like the ideas in his head.

Version two saw several sports represented: rowing, snooker, rugby, cricket, tennis, football—the whole works spread out and jiggled around like a cartoon galaxy around the perimeter. It did add a little more fun and flavour to the scene. Now he just needed some cool lettering to tie it all together.

He scribbled the word "sports" in big block letters, with a football as the 'o' and attempted to mentally reconstruct the lettering into more abstract shapes.

Hmm. Nothing.

He idly rotated the book on the kitchen table in an effort to see the drawing differently by viewing it from a different angle. He squinted his eyes a little and, suddenly, there it was. San Mescalito had just handed him an inspiration. By stylizing the "p" a bit, the word 'sports' looked the same upside-down as it did right-side-up. It was an *ambigram*. And he could make stencils to capture the crisp lines of the classic white-and-black hexagons and pentagons football image in the middle there, and the other shapes around it.

A few tracings later, he had the idea fully baked. Now he just had to scout around to find the perfect place to put it. But that could wait. At last, he felt like he could sleep. He crawled off to bed just before 7:30 a.m. and was nearly asleep when he heard his mum shuffle down the hall toward the kitchen.

* * *

Georgia's phone rang. She raised her head and swept her tousled hair out of her eyes as she looked at the nightstand clock. 1 pm. "Hullo?"

"That was a blast last night, hey?" It was Len.

"You're up early," she said sleepily.

"Mum woke me up at twelve," he replied.

"What's up?" she asked. The excitement in his voice reminded her of how young he was. And still living with his mum!

"Hey, turn on the telly," he said. "It's the BBC One weekend news. They're covering the show. Your eyeball thing is on TV right now!"

Georgia picked up the remote and flipped the channel to BBC One.

"It's being called the 21st century's version of the infamous 14-hour Technicolour Dream, and like that seminal 1967 multi-artist event, the London art scene is once again inspiring poets, artists and musicians...

"Hey, hey—that's your poster right there," she said excitedly as the news coverage of the event focused on the poster as it wrapped up. She muted the volume on the TV. "You're gonna sell some of those now."

"Y'think?"

"Oh for sure. You've got some left, I hope? Gallery size? Oh good. I'll take a few." She grabbed a pencil and scribbled his name. "What'll you sell them to me for? Six quid? Weren't you giving them away just yesterday? I was thinking more like two. I see. All right, three then." She tapped the pencil eraser on the paper like an auctioneer's gavel. "Three it is. If you've got lots, I'll take a couple of dozen. Can you sign them? Yeah, yeah, perfect."

On the other end of the line, Len felt lucky again. This was all gravy, paid for by Robber Bob.

"You were quite a bundle of energy last night," she said, realizing her feet were feeling a little tender after all their dancing. She'd probably been a little *too* friendly to this little puppy.

"I had *so* much fun," he said enthusiastically. "That second band was great. How is it that I've never heard of them before?"

"I think they were called 'Children of Angels', said Georgia. "I've seen their name before but yeah, that was the first time I'd heard them, too. They're from around here, apparently."

"I really dug it—it was *so* hypnotic, with those rotating thread spirals or whatever they were behind them on the screen. And great to dance to. Damn good stuff."

"Yeah, and the songs seemed to just go on forever. I swear, their first piece was like an hour long."

"Honestly, it was better than I thought it would be," he admitted.

"Are you going back tonight?" she asked.

"I dunno. Maybe. Are you?"

"Not me. I've got a big cup of tea here and I'm just going to heat up some leftovers and curl up in front of the telly tonight. If our eyeball guy doesn't sell tonight, I've got to pack it up tomorrow, so there's that."

"I hear ya. I *could* go. I've got a free door pass, but I think I might spend a little time working on my next art piece instead. I had kind of an interesting idea last night."

"I think we all did. That dragon was freaking me out. It kept changing."

"You mean the colours?"

"No, I mean I was trippin' pretty hard on the geometry of the wireframe of that thing. I kept thinking it was breathing. I know, it sounds a bit stupid now."

"Nah, I know what you mean. That shit was first-class."

"And I totally lost track of Alec and the others. Hopefully they weren't looking for me..."

"So," he asked her, "where do you know Alec from?"

"Oh, he's an artist. He comes into my gallery once in a while. I've seen a few of his pieces. Some of them are quite good. A bit uneven, perhaps." She didn't mention that she and Alec had a bit more of a history than that, but she realised that she'd practically said as much.

"Hmm. And you think he's on the level?"

"Meaning what?"

"You know, do you think he's trustworthy?"

"Yeah, I think so. He's pretty secretive. I don't think he's a big-time drug dealer or anything like that. But he's definitely got money."

"Can you drop those posters off at my gallery? It's on Old Street. Really close to here."

"Yes, I know the place. The Smash Gallery. Why's it called *Smash?*"

"Well, we've got a lot of neon. And there's a bar next door. Probably not the ideal location."

"Oh yeah, the neon eyeball thingie was from Smash Gallery. I remember."

It occurred to Georgia that Len apparently hadn't really been listening when she'd mentioned the same piece a few minutes earlier. "I'm hoping to sell that piece tonight. It's a hassle to transport."

"I can imagine. It'll probably sell. It's pretty cool."

"I think so, too," she mused. "I might drop the price a little. So, you'll drop those posters off?"

"I will. Prob'ly tomorrow. I look forward to seeing the place."

"Oh, we're closed tomorrow," she reminded him.

"Sunday. Of course. Um, is Monday afternoon soon enough?"

"Sure. I won't be there, but just leave them with the woman at the counter—her name is Bernice. If you bring an invoice, she'll pay you right away. I'll let her know you're coming. She'll have gloves too, so she won't mess them up."

"Bernice. Got it, thanks."

"All right then. I've gotta go. Cheers."

* * *

Three

Running in a Circle

A few hours later, Len's phone rang.

"Hello?"

"Hello," said a deep voice. "Is this Lenz Design?"

"Yes it is. This is Len. How can I help you?"

"Come out to the front of the building."

Len peeked out the window. A large late-model luxury saloon was double-parked just outside, on the street below. Intrigued, Len slipped on his shoes, grabbed his keys, and went out to see who it was.

As he approached the car, the rear window slid down. It was Alec, alone in the back seat. "Get in," he said as he opened the rear door for Len. "I've got something to show you."

It was at that moment that Len realised that Georgia must have given his phone number and street address information to Alec. "Fair's fair," he thought. After all, she'd given him *her* number.

Alec slid over to make room for him and Len climbed into the back seat of the car, intrigued—an immediately feeling underdressed. Alec was wearing a sports jacket and what appeared to be a starched white shirt. With cufflinks! Len had to hand it to him. Mr. Haircut sure knew how to dress a notch or two better than most folks.

A glance at the "Flying B" bonnet ornament confirmed his hunch that the car was a Bentley. "Nice car," Len said. The driver turned his head.

"Thanks," he said. It was Dal in the driver's seat. "It's a 2012 Bentley Flying Spur. You should never *ever* buy one of these," he warned. They are *crazy* expensive to fix."

"Noted," said Len, quite sure this would never be a problem he'd face.

"Off we go," said Alec to Dal and off they went. The big car plowed ahead like a powerboat.

"We've got a right treat for you," said Dal, as they turned the corner. Len noticed that he was also dressed very well, in what appeared to be a dark blue suit jacket. Len looked down at Alec's expensive-looking leather shoes and fancy wristwatch. The two of them looked like they were heading out to some sort of formal affair. Len was dressed for a trip to the ice cream parlour.

"Yeah, I think you might like this," said Alec, sensing Len's curiosity. "Ah, here it is, up on that wall on the left there." Dal pulled the car over and parked in view of the wall.

It looked, to Len's eyes, like a riff on the old Pink Floyd *Wish You Were Here album* cover, in the style of a two-frame cartoon. In frame #1, an executive was shaking hands with a gleaming chromium robot. In frame #2, the robot was in the position of the executive, shaking mechanical hands with another robot. The caption read: "If you can be replaced by a machine, you should be."

"Oh wow, yeah," Len remarked. "I've never seen that piece before. Pretty nice one, too. Who's it by?"

"Me, actually," said Alec, "...with a little help from Dal here and Johnnie. It's our little warning to middle managers everywhere. We banged it out after we left the Moloko gig last night. We were done by sunrise."

Dal turned his head and grinned. "Pretty fockin' epic, eh?"

"No shit..." Len marveled at the design and detail. "How did you get up there?" he asked.

"We had some ladders and a van, thanks to Dal," said Alec.

"And a hell of a lot of spraycans and stencils too," added Dal.

"Well, bravo, guys," said Len. He turned to Alec. "It's really next-level stuff. My hat's off to you. And nobody saw you doing all this?"

"Nah, we put a curtain up and I had a couple o' good lookouts."

Dal grinned. "We were invisible," he whispered mysteriously.

"We'll head back to Len's place now, Dal."

"Gotcha." Dal threw the car into gear and pulled back onto the street.

"So..." said Alec, "that's kinda what we—my crew and I—do," he explained. "I call 'em the Dream Team."

"'Cause we only do the paintin' stuff at night," chuckled Dal.

"And I was wondering if you wanted to...y'know, be a part of it. Join my crew.... What do you think?"

"Hm. Let me think about it a little," said Len, cautiously.

Alec didn't mention it, but he'd had Dal and Johnnie tailing Len for most of the week. He was finally satisfied that Len was no more and no less than he claimed to be.

"Listen," said Alec. "We're getting together at the Old Stag's Head this Tuesday evening—me, Dal and Johnnie. Oh, and I think your dance partner Georgia will be there, too," he added casually. "You two looked like you were getting along rather well the other night. And Paulie and Petra might be there, too. Why don't you drop by and we can have a few laughs and maybe that'll help you decide—what do you say?"

"Yeah, all right," said Len.

"All right, we'll see you there at eight o'clock sharp. You know the place, right?"

"That's the place on Holywell? Yeah, no problem. 8 p.m. Tuesday. See you there."

That was the thing about Alec, Len realised. He was always very specific in getting people to do what he wanted. It was like a kind of Jedi mind power.

And Dal might be an idiot, but apparently he's an idiot with a fancy car and a big van and pots of money. So that started to make some sense, too.

"Oh, by the way," said Alec, "what size of hoodie do you wear?"

"A medium," said Len. An unexpected question, to be sure.

* * *

On Tuesday, Len arrived at Holywell Row well before eight. He was better dressed now but worried that appearing before anyone else arrived might be seen as an attempt to upstage the scene. Maybe Alec had a specific seating area in mind. Hopefully they wouldn't all be dressed in baggies and hoodies now. That would be hilariously awkward, if he were the only one dressed up now. He decided not to risk looking like a grandstander and took a walk around the neighbourhood instead.

There was a small, slightly run-down looking letterpress shop that looked interesting. It was closed, unfortunately. Through the window he could see an old Heidelberg printing press—*very* old school. Len imagined it would have that familiar smell of inks and turps and machine oil, like some of the other machines he'd worked on. Places with classic machines like that didn't do commercial work for cheapskates. They were more often in the business of producing super-deluxe limited editions on fabulous linen-paper and wedding invitations for the obscenely wealthy—not exactly mainstream stuff these days.

Next to it was a nondescript legal office and, on the other side of that, a small neighbourhood café, also closed. Across the way was what looked like a lighting manufacturer, advertising—of all things—custom neon. It seemed highly likely that Georgia would know of this place and was probably even a customer. Len made a mental note to ask her about it when he saw her.

Len checked the time. Ten to the hour. He couldn't think of any good reasons *not* to join the crew. He continued his little walkabout, and figured that once around the block would bring him back to the door of the pub at just about the right time. The far end of the block on Holywell was pretty drab, though, with its unnamed office spaces, a generic-looking office supply store, and some sheet metal storefront covers. This was definitely on the outskirts of the 'interesting' part of the neighbourhood, he thought. The street on the other side leading back to the pub was even more corporate. Hopefully the pub wouldn't be full of corpos.

At precisely eight o'clock, he opened the door and strode into the pub. Being a Tuesday night, it wasn't especially busy. Fortunately, the crew had managed to secure a table. Sitting at a long table along the back wall, he saw 'tall guy.' Tall equals Paul. Ah yes, Paulie. And that must be Petra. For some reason, he had no trouble remembering that name. As Len squeezed through the crowd alongside the bar, he spotted Johnnie and Dal. And, heading to the table from the other direction was Alec.

"Hey, everybody, here's Len," announced Alec. "Len, let me introduce you to Paulie and the lovely and talented Petra."

Petra was really a striking young woman. She struck Len as Street Art, personified—skater punk hair and makeup, funky urban style, great tattoos, and wild graffiti colours. With positively electric eyes. They were a stylish bunch, this lot.

"Pleased to meet you and nice to see you all again," said Len with a smile as he sat down. "Have you guys been served yet?"

"Nah, we just got here," replied Paulie. "Glad to meet you."

"Perfect timing, well done," said Alec, still dressed to the nines as he had been earlier in the afternoon. Len felt a little self-conscious, as if these were his job interview clothes.

"You're the handbill guy, right?" said Paulie, remembering Len from their brief conversation at Hoxton Square.

"Yeah. I do a few other things, too."

"Indeed," said Alec. "And that is precisely why he is with us here tonight."

As he often did, Alec played up the revelation of a new plan like a hammy Shakespearean actor. He laid his arms purposefully on the table with his palms up and motioned with his fingers. "Gather 'round, thou faithful few and let me tell you what steeps here in the teapot of my mind."

Alec explained that he was looking for ideas for their next big piece. The theme, he said, is 'missing.' "So send me your ideas for an image that captures this idea in a provocative way. I want it to communicate the concept of missing out, missing the point, missing absent friends, missing the dearly departed, missing the action, and so on. Okay?"

They bandied around some ideas until Alec raised his hand and the group went silent. "Send them to me by noon on Monday," he said quietly, "and if there are any release candidates, I'll bring them along to our meeting here next Tuesday."

"I'm thinking the picture itself could be the thing that's missing," mused Paul. "Like *it's* been stolen, right? That raises the whole issue of community ownership, property, and theft, yeah?"

"Oh, that would be awesome," said Dal. "Just a painting of a hole in the wall. So if the greedies do abscond with it, it'll still look the same. Haha!"

Petra said: "Maybe we could have a picture of people sawing it out? It's very recursive. I like it."

As he sketched the ideas out in his piece book, the concept was solidifying in Paul's mind. "...And if some greedy bastard cuts the thing out and tries to sell it, that caption will be right on the nose below an actual hole in the wall, too. Even if they patch it."

"Diabolical!" said Johnnie.

"And," Paul continued, "if they cut out the MISSING text, too, the piece will become entirely abstracted, but will still have a meaningful title and a conceptual presence."

"Despite sounding deeply pretentious, I have to admit I like where you're going with this," said Alec.

"Boggles the mind," added Dal. "That's a two-teabag idea, that one."

"There's a fascination paradox in there—I like it," declared Johnnie. "It says a lot even when not saying anything. I've always liked things that are meaningful *because* of their absence."

"But only if you know about what *was* there—what's supposed to be there," surmised Paul.

"It's an intriguing idea, especially if *missing* the point is the point of the art."

"Pretty arrogant to tell people they're missing the point," warned Georgia.

"Do you want to paint it?"

"Paint what? A photo-realistic picture of a hole in a brick

wall? Or the perforated outline of a cut-out box that says "missing' as if you're supposed to cut them out or collect them...?"

"That's weird. You want to paint *that*?"

"Nah," decided Paul. "It's one of those ideas that really isn't ideally suited to paint on a wall. It would only look convincing from a very narrow range of viewpoints. One, really. And photo-realism would be a challenge at best."

"If only there were some sort of programme we could use as if it were a photo shop," joked Petra, in mock awe.

"For that reason, I don't think the piece itself is necessarily the art. The art could be the perfect photograph of the perfect view of the piece. And is reality or a photo-realistic rendering more important in that context?"

"Now you sound like fockin' Bailie, teaching us that *shite* about rendering and all," said Dal, rolling his eyes.

"As he does," agreed Johnnie.

"I think you're too quick to dismiss paint," said Georgia. "You could have a series of historical images with discomforting elements that provide an additional layer of context, or provocative depictions of world leaders looking really uncomfortable as they're sitting in a hovel somewhere, sitting on grubby crates and barrels."

"Ha."

"Or a series consisting of complex pictures with many obviously missing items. It's fun to think of increasingly reductionist ways of expressing the idea. A missing sock. A missing chromosome...."

"...but with little 'this item is missing' placeholder markers." offered Johnnie. Len could relate to this little desktop publishing in-joke.

Paul was in full-on art philosophy mode now. "Anyway, my point was that the environment itself inspires the art. The viewer is the solution to the equation. The art doesn't exist without that interaction. In *this* case, at least."

"Dynamic art that interacts with its environment was your final project, so this *is* kind of your thing," Petra teased.

"We could do a multi-panel cartoon spoof of Schrödinger's is-it-or-isn't-it thought experiment, but with art instead of a cat," she suggested. "Or art *of* the two cat-states, ha. Schrödinger's Art. Simultaneously art and not art. Missing and not missing."

"Or go full-on Marcel Duchamp: This is/is not Schrödinger's Hat."

"Get it?!"

"I'm pretty sure no one else would find that as funny as we do."

"I thought MISSING might work as a milk carton," Johnnie said. "I'd like to do something like this as a proper art installation piece, with a sort of periscope mirror setup inside the milk carton to make the 'missing person' come alive as an animated milk carton photo. The projector could be hidden below the milk carton, or it might even be possible to run the projection from a small computer and battery embedded right inside the carton. It would be so cool to have a series of milk cartons where each of the characters are back-projected onto their own milk carton, so these missing people could be seen as living people. They can tell or show their own story, you know?"

"I'd like to see us have some fun with the idea by showing something humorous that ties in with the theme of 'missing.' You know, like a Royal Guard with his bearskin hat missing, looking suspiciously at a fluffy black dog, or something like that."

"We could produce a series of pieces providing social commentary while still making them entertaining to look at. Something like a B-52 bomber that drops Crayolas instead of bombs... 'Missing' could be signified by coloured splat marks below the plane."

"...or what about a gunner taking aim at a whole swarm of Mary Poppinses?

'Missing' in this case is the punchline."

"Ha!"

"We're getting off track here folks," Alec cautioned them, "which reminds me...."

He pulled a backpack from underneath the table onto his lap. "I've got something here..." he said as he opened the pack, "...that commemorates our recent success with the robots mural." He held up a gray hoodie with a screenprinted image of an "I'm not a robot" reCAPTCHA dialog box.

 I'm not a robot 

"I hope I've got the right sizes for everyone here," Alec said as he handed them out.

"It's like a humanist manifesto," said Petra. "I like it. Thanks!" She and Johnnie both held theirs up to their chests.

"I love it," declared Johnnie.

Petra was his best friend. She was always there for him. And she always had been. She was a year older than he was and was like the big sister he never had. They'd walked to elementary school together and secondary school, too. They smoked their first cigarette together and coughed and laughed. They'd cried together, grown up together. Even counting height. She'd often ask to try on his jackets. They always looked better on her. And then Paul was in the picture and suddenly the two of them were going out. Funny how life changes like that, Johnnie thought.

"And I know that Len wasn't directly involved, but his fab poster helped pave the way for our success that night, so there's one here for you too, Len. Congratulations to you all."

As he got to know the members of the crew, Len learned that Paulie and the two other art-school guys had just submitted their final projects during the past week and they were now officially on summer break. Johnnie explained that they would, however, be returning to the School of Fine Art in the fall and, as he described it, "collecting bottles and having bake sales until then to pay for it."

Johnnie insisted that Petra tell her story about why she'd been kicked out of that school just a little over one year ago.

"On a charge of sabotage, no less!" added Paul.

"Yeah, we've got a criminal mastermind in our midst," joked Johnnie.

Petra explained: "I had suggested a multimedia art piece for my final design class project that involved a series of images inspired by a grand piano. The instructor liked the idea and had given me a note confirming that I had permission to inspect the music department's piano." The story, Petra explained, took a dark turn when she was confronted by the school's elderly music instructor, who was surprised to see "this punk rocker and complete stranger" lifting the lid of her precious grand piano. The instructor immediately jumped to the conclusion that this young hooligan was, in her words, "sabotaging" the piano and she forcibly grabbed Petra by the shirt collar and ripped it.

"You..." Petra exclaimed, but bit her tongue before she finished the sentence. She was in the right here, after all, and didn't want to get in trouble.

The instructor glared back. "*You* will come to the office with me *now*," she insisted, but Petra just waved the note at her.

"I will *not*. I have explicit permission to be here." The teacher grabbed the note from her hand and, unfortunately, Petra never saw it again.

As Petra sat in front of the Dean, the teacher fabricated a story that Petra had called her a bitch and called for her to be expelled. Petra denied this, of course, but it was the teacher's word against hers and, naturally, the teacher prevailed. She denied that the note ever existed—and, unfortunately, some-how managed to dissuade the original note writer from con-firming Petra's innocence. The next thing Petra knew, she'd been expelled—and only 40 days before graduation!

Paul, Johnnie, and a couple of dozen of her other school-mates had lodged protests and even staged a walkout in support of her case, but it was to no avail.

"And so ended my pursuit of a fine arts degree at the school," she said.

"I later discovered how the design class teacher had been persuaded to betray me. As it turned out, someone had broken into the glass display case outside the office of the school and stolen a piece of my artwork that was displayed there. School officials were convinced that I had concocted the stunt myself and vandalised the display to draw attention to myself and increase my artistic notoriety. Good idea," admitted Petra, "but I didn't do it."

"Wow, that's unbelievable," said Len.

"It's an absolutely true story," she swore. "And the irony is that bullshit like that *did* radicalise me to a certain extent. I'm very much more interested in artistic notoriety now, as a result of being double-crossed like that. I got back at them, though. This spring, I taught commercial design at that school, standing in the same goddamned staff room as those bastards who had conspired to kick me out."

"But you never discovered who broke into the display case?"

"Nope, I never did. But I guess someone out there believed my artwork was worth stealing, so that was kind of inspiring, really."

* * *

As he got to know the others in the group better, Len realised that he had to step up his game in a number of areas. Georgia owned her own gallery and a nice car, and was commissioning full-scale artworks and neon sculptures. Paul, Dal, and Johnnie were just a year away from graduating from a fairly prestigious art school. Alec was custom-producing elaborate gifts for his team members—and was being chauffeured around town in a Bentley, for heaven's sake. And Petra was teaching commercial art classes. They each must have dropped at least £150 to attend the Moloko art event. And they all dressed well, but none better than Alec. He had a knack of dressing in a way that said "I'm very successful" that managed to look both casual and sophisticated without appearing fussy or overly fastidious.

"And here I am," thought Len, "dirt-poor and doing the same kind of stuff I was doing in secondary school, running around town putting up posters for affairs I can't even afford to attend." He was tired of standing on street corners handing out flyers and working for peanuts. Tired of doing errands on a bicycle. Guys like that didn't get a second date with a girl like Georgia.

That Friday afternoon, he texted Alec. "I've decided I'll join."

"Great. Drinks tonight to celebrate?"

"F.A.B."

Len wondered if Alec would catch the old Thunderbirds reference.

The reply answered his question. "Will pick up Lady Penelope and rendezvous at twenty hundred hours."

At 8 p.m., the Bentley pulled up outside Len's flat. Len, wearing his best shoes and jacket, was already waiting on the sidewalk. The back door opened, and there was Danielle, with Alec—immaculately dressed, as always—beside her. "Lots of room," said Alec. "Jump in."

Another young woman was in the front seat opposite Dal who, as usual, was driving. She turned to look at Len.

"Hello there," she said with a friendly smile, "I'm Zena. I'm a friend of Alec's."

She had curly dark brown hair and silver earrings. Her smokey eye makeup made for an exotic look that complemented her striking features and clear dark complexion.

"Very pleased to meet you," said Len. "So, is that front seat as comfortable as the ones back here?"

"Oh, it certainly is," she said, revealing good taste in colour-matching with her painted lips and fingernails as she playfully squeezed the upholstery. "This is great, isn't it?"

Dal just smiled. "I thought maybe we'd head off for a drink and a bite to eat before we hit the club, eh? Len is celebrating tonight, so the drinks are on me."

"And what is it you are celebrating tonight, Len?" she asked.

Len didn't know what he should or shouldn't say. He looked to Alec for that.

Alec picked up on it right away. "He's got a new role, with big things ahead. He's on his way to the top, this one."

"Woo!" said Zena, flashing a big smile. Len felt Danielle shifting her position slightly. That padded center area between the seats was probably not very comfortable. He moved closer to the door to give her some more room and saw that she didn't look especially pleased.

The Bentley pulled up outside the restaurant and Dal, very convincingly playing the role of chauffeur, jumped out to open the rear door and helped the ladies out of the car. Alec gave him a wink and a folded banknote. "We'll be exactly two hours," Alec said to him. "See you then," said Dal.

Seeing the way these gorgeous women responded to these luxurious trappings of the good life—the VIP treatment, expensive champagne and gourmet meals—raised feelings that Len had never really thought about much before. But he also realised he was playing the role of wingman here and decided to just go with it.

So, like any good wingman, Len played it cool. He kept things fun, made lots of eye contact, asked lots of questions, and didn't interrupt. He didn't try to lead the conversation anywhere, he just kept everyone included.

As it turned out, the restaurant was a great place to take a date. The ladies headed off to the powder room together—probably a good sign, noted Alec while they were away—and everyone was really impressed by the food. The fact that the girls felt compelled to mention how lavish the washroom was didn't hurt, either. This reminded Alec of a story and, as he filled everyone's glasses, he introduced it as the best stag party he'd ever been to. And it was, he declared, "right in this building, in this room, in fact."

"I had this buddy who was getting married, y' see," he explained, "and we rented this room for our little party. Anyway, you might not have noticed it when we came in, but there's a sign up on the back wall of the main restaurant that says "Washrooms *this way*. So everyone who's lookin' for a washroom has to come by *this* room, see?"

Well, I combined my mad skills in forgery and sign making and I made what you might generously call a counterfeit 'Ladies room' sign for the door of *this* room and put it up on the outside of this door here. And, of course, me and the guys are all in here having a stag party for our buddy. And the ladies would come along looking for the Ladies room and see *our* sign instead...."

"Oh no!" said Zena.

"They'd come in expecting the ladies washroom and then *boom*—a bit of a surprise. They'd look all confused and go 'oh, excuse me, I seem to be in the wrong room' and we'd just roar with laughter."

"Oh, you're terrible! Those poor girls," laughed Danielle.

"It was hilarious! And terrible, yes, we've all learned our lessons, haven't we Len?"

"I dunno, but I'm a bit nervous to go to the men's room now." And they all laughed.

* * *

Alec pulled Len aside and spoke in a quiet voice. "I need your help with something, Len." He looked Len in the eyes. "Have you got some time to do a bit o' work for me?"

Len hadn't mentioned the Moloko fiasco and his other recent client cancellations to anyone yet, so he doubted that anyone knew the extent of his suddenly dire financial status. He didn't want to appear *too* eager, though. "What have you got in mind, mate?"

"D'you think you could make some stencils for me?"

"Stencils? Like silkscreen type stuff or stencils for wall graffiti?"

"Yeah, stuff like that. Maybe two or three colour overlays. Nothin' too complicated."

"Yeah, sounds doable. I like doin' that sorta stuff."

"Yeah, I know mate," Alec grinned. "That's why I'm asking ya."

"What's the idea?"

"I've got some ideas for some new images, and I've made

a few into stencils, but they're a bit rough, y'know? Yours are really next level, so I thought maybe you could do 'em for me. If you have the time, of course."

"Of course."

"I'll pay you for them, naturally. What d'ya think would be reasonable? £50 apiece upon approval, maybe?"

"How many do you want?"

"As many as you can bang out. Twelve to start, maybe? I'll give you the stills from my vids. Some of those crazy crowd scenes from the riots in America are classics in the raw, seriously."

"Yeah, that was bonkers, man."

"I really appreciate this. Oh, one more thing. I want to own the rights to the images I pay you for and I don't want you to discuss this deal with anyone else. No one at all, okay?" He extended his hand. "Deal?"

Len was relieved that this deal seemed to be pretty much above board. No crime, no worries. "Yeah, sure, mate. You send me the stuff, and I'll get to work on it right away."

As he worked on the project, Len couldn't help but wonder if Alec had deals like this with any of the others.

Four

Doors and Windows

Len brought his piece book along to the meeting that week, as he often did. While they were waiting for the server to come to the table, Len opened the sketchbook and flipped through the pages.

"Hey Alec," said Len. "I made a little sketch you might like." He opened the book to a page with a brightly coloured illustration and handed it to Alec.

Alec studied it in silence for a moment that seemed to go on forever. Petra and Paul, who were both wearing their "I'm not a robot" hoodies, leaned over the table for a closer look. "Patience, good people, please." Another long moment passed as he silently contemplated the image. Len was just beginning to feel a little nervous about the expressionless silence when Alec finally moved again. He checked the table to make sure it was dry and then put the book down. "Very cool," he declared. "Can I show it to the others?" Alec asked him.

"Absolutely. Thanks for asking," he said. Len liked being shown a little respect like that. Alec passed the open book to Petra, who studied it for a moment, then smiled and turned it upside-down.

As she raised her eyes, she looked at Len and gave a subtle wink, then rotated the book again.

"Well, aren't you the clever one," said Alec. "Look at that, Dal," he said. "You can read it upside-down *or* right-side-up."

"But why would anybody be looking at it upside down? Are *they* upside down?"

"I don't think that's the point, Dal. Besides, it could be on a table or a wheel or something."

"Or a T-shirt," Len offered.

"It would have to be pretty small to fit on a wheel," grumbled Dal to himself.

Alec suddenly smiled and said: "You know where this would be really perfect? On the ceiling of a tunnel. You could read it going in either direction."

"Omigod, that's brilliant. We should absolutely do that."

"We'll scout around for the perfect place for it," Alec assured him. "But there's one thing we need to do first."

Alec started in with his usual routine: "Gather 'round, for conception is a blessing...."

"First of all," he said, "I'd like to thank everybody for the ideas they sent in. I've reviewed them all and I'm pleased to say that I've finalised the first of the new designs we're going to put up—and I've got the perfect wall to put it on." He paused for dramatic effect.

"You know that new investment bank that's opening up on Hoxton Square... the place on the south side, with the light gray wall?"

Len said, "I know *exactly* the place you're talking about." Paul and Johnnie nodded. Petra just shook her head.

"Well, that north-facing second-storey wall of theirs is where we're gonna put *this*."

With a dramatic flair, he lifted the cover of his binder and showed off the concept sketch.

It was a stencil-art image of a boy and a girl staring at gadget screens. Below the image was the word MISSING.

"This is what it'll look like," explained Alec, "—except much, much larger, of course."

"I like it," said Johnnie. "It suggests both the disconnection from the here-and-now that occurs when people are staring at their screens and there's the 'missing children' idea too…"

"Except *they* are the missing children," mused Len. "Nice."

"Or perhaps their missing their lovely brand-name logo because their parents bought them a cheap piece o' crap knockoff," suggested Dal.

Alec nodded approvingly.

"I wonder if perhaps we could make a more pointed political statement about the pervasive nature of cellphone slavery," said Petra. "Or consumerism in general."

"I think it kinda *does* get that across," countered Paul. 'Missing' also suggests a surveillance angle," he added. "I could see a message about empowering the crowd or taking back the surveillance society with a caption like RECORD EVERYTHING…"

Dal laughed and said: "My first thought when I saw that picture was OBSOLETE. No matter what phone we put up there, it'll be out of date practically before the paint even dries. And *everybody* can relate to that."

Dal was annoyed because the brand new iPhone he'd bought in 2007 had already been discontinued by the very next summer and then, after he bought the brand new model, *that* one was discontinued, too, just this past June. He was also annoyed because his friends sometimes didn't even bother to respond when he said something. That hurt, but he'd learned long ago not to show it. Besides, the way Alec explained it, it was all like an act, and he was being paid for being an actor.

Len seemed to clue in that no one else was going to respond

to Dal, so he followed with "Yeah, it looks like they're staring at a message that says 'Sorry, the update you've selected is not compatible with your device.'"

"Oh man, I hate that," said Dal.

"Same," said Len, raising his glass.

"Maybe we could play up the anarchistic angle with something like *defy*," suggested Johnnie.

"Hm, yes, I like *defy*, it's very strong and anarchic, said Paul. "It really suits the 'socialist realism' style being used here, too."

"Nope. We can't use *defy*, just like we couldn't possibly use *obey*," argued Petra. "It's just too derivative, like a knock-off of—or, depending on your point of view, a reaction to—Shepard Fairey's 'Obey' sticker designs. It ends up looking like art-scene infighting, which I'm fairly sure is *not* the point we're trying to make."

"You're right, Okay, we're going to play a little game here."

Alec handed out pencils and small pieces of paper to everyone. "I want you to write down all the words you can think of that represent some aspect of cellphone culture."

"You mean like 'porn'?" quipped Johnnie. They all laughed.

"Yes. Funny is good, for sure. Words that have more than one meaning, like 'charge' or 'submit' are also good."

"Aww, 'charge' was on *my* list," moaned Dal. "Can I still submit it?"

"Don't worry about duplicates. Just write 'em down."

"I'll order another round," said Alec. "Back in a minute or two...."

"Okay, time's up. Let's have 'em."

Alec mixed the papers up a little and then read the list of suggestions aloud.

Okay, here's what we've got: "Swipe…"

"Ooh, two points for the double meaning there."

"Charge (*triple* meaning there!), share, like, follow, consume, buy, pay, update, upgrade, smash, crash, slave, hack, break, stream, resist, anonymous, record everything…"

"'Resist' works well with that image in a couple of ways, I think," said Paul. "It works as a critical comment about resisting the urge to constantly check your phone, but in the broader social sense, it urges people to resist oppression, resist conformity, and that sort of thing, too."

"I know who submitted that one," Petra teased Paul.

"Not necessarily," said Alec. "There are some duplicates here. Carrying on now… ah-*hem*!" He put the already-read notes in a pile on the table and continued. "…Attack, deny, yield, reject, here's another *resist*, submit, subvert, accept, refuse, pray, prey with an 'e'…"

"Ooh, nice dark one," said Petra. "Resist is very chilly, too."

Alec put the note down rather deliberately and continued. "…Love-slash-hate…"

"Nice one," said Paul. Petra raised her eyebrows and fluttered her eyelashes coyly.

Alec continued reading. "…Consume—oops, already had that one, didn't we?— disconnect, turn off, rethink, zombies, outlaws, fad, obsolete, give, take, open, save, quit, kill, call, talk, pay, play, work… and—last but not least—porn."

"I'll vote for outlaws," put in Petra. "The idea that taking a photo or a video with your phone might make you a police target is just so perfectly dystopian. It's the kind of social commentary that I think we should be focusing on, honestly."

"I still think porn's the funniest, said Johnnie. "And just look at their expressions. PORN!!!"

"All right," said Alec. "Time to vote."

They narrowed down the list to a set of six finalists: Rethink, Disconnect, Resist, Turn Off, Record Everything, and Porn. Alec insisted that 'Missing' had to be on the list too, so it was amended to seven semifinalists.

The list was then voted on twice more while looking at the picture of the blank-faced users to derive a short list of three finalists: *Missing* was narrowly beat out by *Disconnect, Rethink,* and *Resist* and these were deemed to be the captions that added the most meaning to the image. In the end, *Rethink*, it was agreed, demanded the most of the viewer while communicating an essentially positive message. *Rethink* it was.

"So, let's agree on a night. Sunday's the quietest night in terms of police patrols, but Mondays are pretty quiet, too. I'd like to get this thing done this week, either Sunday or Monday. Dal's got the van available for us for either night. What's your preference?"

After a bit of debate about football schedules, it was decided that Sunday would be the perfect night.

"We'll bring the cloak of invisibility to keep it dark, of course."

There was, of course, much to be done before Sunday. Paul and Petra were sent out on bicycles to survey the area for security cameras. As it turned out, there were only two on this block, and they were both facing away from the wall. Then, careful to avoid showing their faces in areas visible to the security cams, Johnnie and Dal scouted the neighbourhood on foot later that week, on the lookout for nosey neighbours, barking dogs, late-night security guards or night watchmen, and other risks.

The second- and third-floor windows south of Hoxton Square were all office spaces; the restaurants at ground level on Rufus Street closed up early in the evenings on Sundays. Fortunately, the building directly opposite the wall was always completely empty at that time of night; it effectively blocked the view from the north, so they only had to worry about traffic from the south.

As usual, Alec instructed them to make careful notes about the heights of the walls and angles of the roofs they'd have to scale. Alec quickly realised this was something of a core competency for Len. He was highly adept at planning and logistics-related tasks. Alec laid out the master plan and Len filled in the details on the most efficient way to pack and unload the van. He had good ideas on where to park it, how to take advantage of one-way streets, and emergency escape routes. He suggested they look for evidence of home-less people in the park to the north who might pose a problem and considered potential line-of-sight issues that might be posed by passing pedestrians.

Len also suggested making copies of number plates legit-imately used on a van of the identical type and colour to the one they used to avoid being identified. That way, he reasoned, a routine police computer check would show the plate matching the type of vehicle and would not appear suspicious. They stuck magnetic sheets with the "cloned" number plate images over the van's real plates, white on the front and yellow on the rear. They even planned where they would stash a couple of sets of alternate hats and hoodies, in case they needed to make a getaway on foot and needed a quick disguise.

As Alec often said, it's all in the planning. At the final prep meeting, Alec handed out little folded paper packets to the crew containing carefully measured microdose portions of chocolate-flavoured synthemesc. It sharpened the senses and made ridiculous risks seem only slightly superhuman. It was the perfect thing to be on when you're hanging by a rope above a freeway.

"There we are," Alec said, as he handed one to Georgia. "Just a microdose this time. We don' want no breathey walls, do we?"

Georgia pocketed hers but decided she would do the job without it. She remembered her younger self telling Alec her philosophy about art and life in general. "Money is the worst reason to do anything," she had declared. How times had changed.

That Sunday night, the van pulled up behind the building. Dal got out and stood guard near the rear doors of the van as the rest of the crew quickly and quietly got the ladders set up and hauled the equipment and tarp up to the roof on the east side of the building.

Len opened the passenger-side door and leaned into the

vehicle. "Just checking..." he said as he closed it again. Dal then moved the van away from the site.

The 'cloak of invisibility' was a large tarpaulin that covered a building wall. In this case, it was hung on a frame and hoisted up the east wall on ropes. Alec and the crew used it to hide their ladders and scaffolds while they taped up their stencils and completed their spray paintings.

And it worked just as perfectly as it always had. To the casual observer or a drive-by law enforcer, it looked like just another blank wall. And it was opaque enough that the crew could have lights inside to work in the early mornings after the pubs and clubs closed, when the streets were quietest.

A few hours later, the ladders, ropes, and equipment came down, the cloak was rolled up, the emergency disguise hats and hoodies were retrieved from their hiding places and the fake number plates were removed. They all piled back into the van. This job was done.

"I could totally go for some shawarma right about now," Paul declared. "Oh, me too," said Johnnie. "Anybody want to hit the all-night café?" Georgia asked. "Sorry, I can't," said Dal. "Alec and I have got to get the van emptied out and it's getting pretty late."

"Well, can you just drop us off at my place?" Georgia asked him. "We'll go in my car."

"Is that OK with you, Alec?" asked Dal.

"Yeah, that works. Thanks for asking."

By the time they got to Georgia's not-quite-under-the-bridge house, everyone was fully engrossed in their favorite food fantasies. They bade farewell and goodnight to Dal and Alec, switched cars and off they went.

Georgia's old BMW bounced along, with Petra squeezed in the middle between Paul and Johnnie in the two back seats and Len in the front passenger seat. A few blocks east of Shoreditch station, the car suddenly veered to the right.

"Uh oh," said Georgia. "I think we have a tyre problem. Feels like the front right. Hang on...."

She pulled the car over and everybody got out to look. Fortunately, a light from across the street illuminated that side of the car. "Omigod," she said when she saw the wrinkled tyre.

"No worries," said Len. "Do you have a car jack?"

"Yeah, I do. It's an old-fashioned scissor jack, but it does the trick," she said as she opened the boot. "Oh shit!" There was no spare tyre. "Oh no, I forgot to put the spare tyre back in the car."

While Georgia was busy berating herself for being such an idiot, Len found the tyre-iron in the boot. He then positioned the jack under the frame of the car and began winding it up.

"Hm," said Paul, "There are a few towing and recovery type places that have 24-hour tyre service. We'll just have to look up one of those. We'll get this taken care of."

"Maybe I should just call Alec?"

"No, no, they're busy unloading."

Johnnie was scrolling through listings on his phone. "Here, I've found a 24-hour service number. Just a minute." He held the phone to his ear. "Hello. Yes, we've had a tyre blow out and we either need it fixed or a replacement, I guess. Uh huh. Could you repeat that, please? Just a minute."

He held the phone to his chest. "He's asking what kind of car do we have?"

"I'll talk to him," said Georgia.

"It's a 1986 BMW E28. Yes, I'll hold." There was a long pause. "Uh huh. that's right. Three days? Ooh, that's not good. Can I just buy a replacement tyre? Oh dear. OK. I'll call you back."

"They say they can't get it repaired or replaced before Wednesday."

"Well, that's no good," Len mumbled as he struggled to loosen a stubborn lug bolt on Georgia's car. At last all of the bolts were removed and the wheel came off.

"There's gotta be some other tyre repair place that's open," suggested Petra.

Johnnie looked through the slats of a metallic fence surrounding an auto repair yard across the street.

"Hey, hey hey—look over here. Isn't that the same kind of car you've got?"

Georgia peered through the slats. "It's certainly similar. But we can't get in there."

"Oh, I don't know. Doesn't look too hard. I don't see any cameras. No killer dogs."

"I'm not going over those pointy stabby things."

"We don't have to. Look at the mailboxes there."

To the right of the picket fence was a metal gate. It also looked more than a bit dangerous to climb over. But just to the right of *it* were a pair of waste bins and a small section of fence adjoining the wall. On this part of the fence, a pair of mailboxes were affixed, as convenient a set of steps as a crew of slightly stoned desperados could ever ask for.

"I think we could hop over there pretty easily," suggested Paul.

Georgia looked skeptical. "And do *what*?"

"I was thinking we'd swap them *our* wheel for theirs. It *is* an auto repair yard, after all. They'll be able to deal with a flat tyre. Heck, leave them some money if you want."

I'm not *that* much of an altruist."

"Don't upscale cars like BMWs have wheel locks?"

"Mine didn't. I don't think any of the older ones came from the factory with them. With a little luck, we'll be able to get that wheel off without too much trouble."

Paul climbed the fence and Len handed him over the jack and the tyre iron. A few minutes later, he returned and lifted the wheel up to Len, who stood on the trash bin and leaned over the fence to retrieve it. "No wheel locks on that one, either. I took it off the side of the car facing the wall," he said. "They'll be less likely to notice it right away."

Len handed the flat tyre over the fence and Paul disappeared behind the donor car. A few minutes later, he returned with the tyre iron and the jack. "All done on this side."

Len and Johnnie both stood on the waste bin and reached over the fence to help him back over the fence while Georgia and Petra held the bin steady. Then Len jacked up Georgia's car one last time and he and Paul bolted the new wheel into place.

They lowered the car to the ground and threw the tools back in the trunk. "Next stop: shawarma!"

Later, at the restaurant, they raised their glasses in a toast. "It was a dodgy plan and a petty crime, but it was successful," said Georgia. "Thank you all."

Finally, with their plates empty and stomachs full, they paid their bills and squeezed back into the car, looking forward to being dropped off at their respective homes.

* * *

It was only about an hour before dawn by the time Len got home. He took a look at a photo he'd taken earlier. It was a closeup of the van's registration papers.

* * *

As he often did after a paint job was done, Alec reflected on what had gone well, and what could have been better. This time, it was the quality of the work that really stood out. He was glad that Petra had been part of the crew this time. He'd met After Midnight and her through Georgia. She seemed smart and was an undeniably talented painter. And she was a very stylish girl. But she had been increasingly unavailable over the past few months—probably due to her burgeoning relationship with Paulie.

Even after Petra and After Midnight eventually broke up, the two of them remained friendly with Alec and Georgia. It wasn't until Georgia met Mr. Wrong and broke off their relationship (to get married, for God's sake!) that the weekend parties with Petra and After Midnight ended.

That was around the time he was still working in his dad's shop, when a man in paint-splattered clothes came to the front counter with an odd proposition. "Do any of you know where I can find someone who can draw?"

"Allie here can draw," his father said. "What've you got in mind?"

"Well," the man explained, "I've got some old templates here that are getting all ripped and I need to replace them. And I'm not an artist myself, so I thought, 'why not update the designs a bit while I'm at it?' So that's what I'm after: replacements for *these.*"

He spread out the tattered templates on the shop table and Alec suddenly realised: he recognised them. He recognised them *all. This* was the guy who painted those terrible Christmas decorations on all the shop windows around town.

The guy who apparently goes around and signs people up in *August*. And now he wants to pay *me* for new designs. What to do? Should I tell this no-talent hack to take a hike or take his money and support his business?

Alec thought for a moment and decided: he *would* take the man's money and give him an improved set of designs. He reasoned that he'd rather see *his* designs all over the city than those ugly ones.

But still, as he pocketed the man's cash, the question nagged at him: *Did I do the right thing?*

This question got him thinking. How did this man of obviously limited artistic talent manage to sell so many window paintings? He concluded that it ultimately came down to two things: having a price customers would be willing to pay, and getting the customers signed up before anyone else did.

The first of the two seemed the one where improvement was needed most, so Alec worked on developing designs with stencils or roll-on techniques that could be produced quickly and reliably. But the more he thought about it, the more he saw the genius in the talentless man's business model. He got other people to supply the designs, and capitalised on their work.

Alec opened up his piece book and took one last look at his 'old' signature. He drew a large X across the page and turned the page. It was time for a fresh start with a new image. A new name, with a new style. Something with street cred. It needed to be something fresh, representing a new attitude. It needed to speak the language of those in the street art scene.

Something like Roady or Streetly or...*Alley*. Alley! It had been hiding in plain sight all along.

He decided that the imagery of the alleys would be his key iconography. The bins, the bricks and cobbles. The steel doors, wire fences, and barred windows. The strangers in the shadows. The pigeons, cats and rats. They all spoke to him.

"Well, look who's up at last. And it's still morning. Fancy that. You had a late night, did you?" said Alec's mum as he stepped into the morning glare of the kitchen.

"Why, yes I did—and thank so much you for asking," said Alec, yawning.

"Would ya like some toast, Allie? You look like you need a cuppa tea."

"No thanks, I think I'll just make some coffee."

"Sorry son, I think your dad's finished off the last o' the bag this morn'. I'll get some more when I go off to the shops this afternoon."

"Do you think you're going to need a new binder or more coloured pencils or anything like that, son?"

"Um, yes, markers. I need markers. Wide ones if possible. Wider the better. Whatever colours they've got. Blue and red if they've got them, preferably."

"You'll need thick paper for that," she warned. "You'll ruin that book o' yours if you draw in it with them."

"It's all right mum. I'll use cardboard or somethin'."

"All right; I'll see what I can find. Blues an' Reds."

* * *

Five

A Small Estate

Alec was in the kitchen when his cell phone rang with the special ringtone reserved for private calls. He looked at the time. 1:30 p.m. He stepped into the hall, headed toward his room and answered the phone as he clicked the door shut. It was the third ring. Not ideal.

"Hello Angel," said the voice. "It's Duckie. It's very important that I see you immediately. Are you at home?"

"Yes."

"Can I pick you up in 10 minutes?"

"I'll be ready, out in front."

"Don't be late."

Duckie always insisted on meeting Alec at the corner, or on the side street.

"You can't be too careful," she had warned him. "You never know who's watching."

Alec was waiting on the sidestreet near the corner when the limo—a Daimler DS420 with an elegant silver-over-blue paint job and tinted windows—pulled around the corner and slowed to a halt. The door opened and Alec slid into the back seat.

"Hello Duckie," he said cheerfully.

"I'll get right to the point," she said. "I'm *very* disappointed to learn that you've chosen to disobey the prime directive."

"I have no idea what you're talking about."

"Don't play stupid with me," she snapped. "You know very well that you disobeyed a specific order never to alter a previously approved design without express permission."

"Nobody liked the caption and everyone voted for what was agreed was a superior alternative," Alec explained.

"Frankly, I couldn't care less if there is a superior alternative," said Duckie sternly. "This is *not* a democracy. Great art does not come from a committee. It requires a singular vision, a powerful voice and a consistent style. If you can't deliver that, tell me now and I'll find someone else who can."

"But—" Alec began. She raised a finger and he was instantly silenced.

"Can I count on you to deliver that?" she repeated.

"Yes," he said dully.

"Now you listen to me. I need you to tell me that you completely understand that *any deviation whatsoever* from the approved plan is strictly forbidden."

"I completely understand that any deviation whatsoever from the approved plan is strictly forbidden," said Alec quietly.

"Good, I'm glad we've straightened that out. You won't be paid for that job of course," she said.

Alec briefly entertained the idea of proposing a redo effort, but he knew her philosophy on leadership wouldn't allow that. "Now, how are the plans for our next project going?" It was when Duckie said words like 'project' and 'whatsoever' that her posh 'Received Pronunciation' accent seemed strongest.

"Everything is ready to go," Alec assured her. "We are scheduled to meet at 8 p.m. tomorrow night to finalise everyone's action items and positions. I do not anticipate any problems."

"You need to pull this one off flawlessly," she cautioned him. "We have the next book ready and waiting for it—and a buyer for the reproduction rights as well."

"We'll take care of it."

"See that you do. Good luck, Angel."

* * *

Alec locked the door to the bathroom and stood in front of the mirror. He shaved and carefully trimmed his sideburns. He put on a shirt. Off it came again. He tried on another, then a third. He had to focus. He had to get things back on track with Duckie. He needed to think of a way to inspire the team into creating a truly great work. He had to visualize success in order to manifest it. He needed a....

Thump thump thump

His concentration was interrupted by the sound of a fist pounding on the bathroom door.

"You still in there? Come on and help your mum with the groceries," Alec's dad said from the other side of the door. "I'm off to work. She's downstairs at the front."

"I'll be right there."

When Alec finished bringing in the groceries, he sat in a chair at the kitchen table. There was a folded copy of *The Daily Mirror* on the other side of the table. Alec flipped it around to read it and then... paused. "There's an idea," he said to himself.

He reflected on how all the paths he'd taken so far in his life had somehow converged to *this*. Today was one of those days where the path suddenly looked like it might be a dead end. Having the business relationship with Duckie so suddenly at risk was stressful in a way that was unlike anything he could remember. There was no way he was going to let the single best business arrangement he'd ever had slip away.

They'd met a couple of years earlier at an art event his dad had been involved with.

It had been his custom screen-printed "I ♥ STREET ART" shirt that had initially caught her attention.

"I like your shirt," this woman had said as they waited in line with their drink tickets. She was attractive and exceptionally well dressed. She looked to be in her late forties or possibly early fifties. Alec found it hard to tell when a woman like that wears the right kind of makeup.

"Why, thank you," said Alec, as politely as he could. "I designed and produced these myself."

"You don't say," she replied, her posh accent revealing itself. "So, you're a clothing designer?"

"Shirts and hoodies mostly," he replied. In fact, those were the only two clothing items he'd ever produced. But Alec had learned that talking up one's achievements as part of some grander plan was the key to getting ahead with the money types. "Pleased to meet you," he said, extending a hand. "My name is Alec. My main business," he said nonchalantly, "is print-making. I do original works, large pieces for corporate clients, commissions and that sort of thing. And I'm working on a series of street art pieces. Hence the shirt," he smiled as he reached the front of the line. "Heineken, please."

"I'm very interested in learning more about those large-scale works you mentioned," she said. "By the way, you can call me Duckie."

"White wine, please," she said to the bartender.

"Well, my dear Duckie," he said with a smile, "I'd be happy to tell you all about them, but first, I simply must know. How did you ever acquire such a delightful name?"

"It's a rather long story," she replied, "but the short version is that it's a derivative of a nickname I used to have. As it is, my friends call me Duckie. And I do hope we can be friends."

In fact, Duckie was a family nickname—a childish deriv-ative of 'Duchess,' which is what her father used to call her. "It's just one title below the monarch," dad explained. "Like princess but even better."

"Gee, it's too bad you didn't tell me *your* rather long story, as I had a *really* long one all set to tell," he teased her.

"Did you bring a car here?" she asked him, seemingly changing the subject.

"No," said Alec. "I live nearby."

"Well, I'll tell you what," she said. "I've got a car and a driver here. You come along and be my guest at dinner, and you can tell me the whole story then. Deal?"

"Deal," he said.

"I'll be ready to go in twenty minutes. I need to have a few words with someone. Will you meet me outside in twenty?"

"I'll be there," he assured her.

Precisely twenty minutes later, the front door of the gallery opened and Alec stepped outside. She was already waiting there. "Ah, grand," she said when she saw him.

"Perfect timing. Here's the car." A man stood at the side of a silver and blue car and opened the rear door as they approached. "This is Bill," she said.

"Bill, Alec will be coming along with us for dinner."

"Very good, madame."

Along the way, they discussed some of the pieces they'd seen at the afternoon's gallery event. Duckie explained that she was a friend of the couple that owned the gallery and was a patron there and at a few other galleries.

The car turned onto a winding street in NW3 and finally came to a stop at a black wrought iron gate in front of a large house on Redington Road near Hampstead Heath. Like many of the other houses in the area, it was a well-kept manor style brownstone building with a tidy hedge pressed up against the ironwork and brick walls along the street. The gate opened and the car pulled around the front door of the house.

"Ah, here we are at last," she said as Bill opened the rear door of the car for them.

She said she wanted to learn more, but it soon became clear she wanted more than that. Over a meal of Cornish hen, roasted vegetables, and caviar, he learned about her interest in art investment, and of the differences between primary, secondary, and auction markets.

Indeed, Alec had never been exposed to this more insular and rarified world of high-end art; his primary exposure to the gallery scene had been to the "affordable art" fairs the galleries he worked with often co-sponsored. And then there were, of course, the "vanity fairs," where you had to pay for your own exhibition space.

She poured him another glass of wine and invited him to come and see her art collection. It wasn't long before the tour led to her bedroom. She asked, "Do you understand the meaning of the word *discretion*, Alec?"

"Yes, I'm sure I do," he replied.

"I have a business proposition for you," she said. At first, Alec wasn't sure if she was serious or not. She was. "I would like to commission a piece, and possibly, a number of pieces from you at a price we both agree is fair. Are you interested?"

"The prices may differ, depending on the pieces, I presume?"

"Of course. And as a condition of sale, I will own it and you will profit. It's a simple sales arrangement. An agreement in writing, shall we say?"

"Not to put it too bluntly, but what sort of price would seem fair to you?"

"Well," she began, "assuming a significant number of pieces were to be sold and upon my acceptance of each piece, we would also have to deduct costs for various aspects of the production and sale. I have it all written down here."

She opened a slim brown leather briefcase and placed a

contact in front of him. "You can take a look and sign it when you're ready."

As he paged through the contract, she summarised the key points. "Each piece will be a limited edition to which I will hold the exclusive rights."

"How many prints or copies does each edition contain?"

"Precisely ten. No more, and no less. Can you agree to that? That number is specified here in writing..." she said, glossing over the fact that the contract actually contained a blank line where any number could be specified. "...in the contract as the number of pieces you agree to sell. To me."

"And what does a piece consist of?"

"Two or more functional stencils and/or colour separations and a reproduction rights sales agreement. The stencil, the surface material, all intellectual property and all physical rights are sold as agreed here."

"You can read the details here before you sign." The contract was, in fact, quite comprehensive—one might say recklessly aggressive—in terms of claiming intellectual property rights. Alec was signing away all present and future rights, in all present and future media formats in perpetuity. Not the sort of thing one should sign without reading.

"This agreement also covers the media, paints or other colourants, plus associated costs and materials I will pay for. And of course, I have to like it. Let's call it a patronage agreement, you sell them to me and we're all happy."

"That's what an agreeable arrangement is all about." said Alec, numbers running through his head, when they oughtn't to have been.

"I want you to understand one thing very clearly, Alec: if I commission a piece from you and I approve the design, you do not change the design without my express permission. No second chances. Is that crystal clear?"

"Understood," said Alec. "I suppose each edition will have to have a different valuation."

"Yes, I should think so. The complexity and the marketability of the design, the amount of time it takes to produce, materials costs, and so on—they are all relevant here. But there many other variables, not all of which you can control. Security and safety concerns, changing market conditions, and that sort of thing. Nevertheless, you'll have to come up with a firm number for each piece. We can't have miscellaneous expenses getting out of hand."

"So, let's be practical about this. Let's begin by assuming you will produce for me two pieces per month. Is that a reasonable assumption?"

"I think so," Alec said.

"Good. Now, how much money would you like to make per month? Would £8,000 be enough? That's above the average wage in the UK, as you may know."

He thought about it for a moment. No sense in being too hasty to accept a wealthy person's first offer.

"I couldn't afford to pay for my production costs on that," said Alec. He had an idea that he could pay his friends to do some of the work but thought it best to keep this notion to himself.

"Look, I don't want to play cat and mouse with you over the price. If you can't do it for £8,000, I'll go find someone who can. Until then, you give me a figure that works for you and I'll consider it."

Alec sensed that this was just a tactic on her part, designed to alarm him into accepting a lowball offer. He knew that £8,000 was practically chump change when one is talking about selling all rights to a major piece, never mind two.

"It's got to be something more like 14K," he insisted.

"That would be lovely, I'm sure," said Duckie, blithely. "But we all have budgets we must adhere to, my dear boy. I'm willing to offer you 8,000 pounds a month for two major pieces, plus their accompanying rights and signed print editions. Take it or leave it."

Alec decided to press the price issue a little more. "Well," he said, "that price wouldn't allow me to be able to afford any workshop space, which is running at about a thousand pounds per month these days. Plus equipment and insurance. And materials. And upkeep. Without a proper workshop for print production, that would mean the pieces would be smaller and less valuable, I suppose. Yeah, bit of a shame not to have a proper workshop. Better productions come from better production facilities, and those would of course incur additional costs."

"Oh, for God's sake," said Duckie. "So, £9,500 a month would be sufficient to cover both you and your expenses?"

"Yes, I could make that work," said Alec, looking up prices of rental spaces on his phone.

Shoreditch High Street Creative Studio Office
130 sq ft - Hackney
from £30 per day

"Well, I'll be expecting very good work for that sort of money."

He smiled. "Of course."

Alec knew that most of the street artists around Shoreditch didn't get paid at all for their work. He figured it would be easy enough to find a few willing to help him out in exchange for beers, pizzas, and the occasional recreational drug. If he played his cards right, he should be able to hang on to most of that money, or at least enjoy spending it on the finer things in life.

"I think that would seem fair to me," he said. "What about cost-of-living increases over time, rent increases, and those sorts of things?"

"This is a three-year contract I'm offering you, with the possibility of extension at the end of that period. We can discuss rent increases and whatnot at that time if you like. But not before."

She emphasised that this amount would be the maximum per month, with the possibility of it being less, if the deliverables were not acceptable. In any event, she made it clear that any monies he was paid in advance were still drawn from the monthly total and that the arrangement was terminable at any time without notice, provided that all terms of the agreement and outstanding commitments have been met.

"I suppose you realize that having an arbitrary ceiling on the price will limit the scope or the scale of this idea of yours. I don't want to preclude the possibility of doing some really big pieces. Do something really outrageous, you know? The *Big Ideas.*"

"Well, yes, in a nutshell, that's exactly what I'm interested in," she said. "It's essentially the ideas I want to be paying you for. You could make a tidy profit, I should say, if you can find other people willing to sell pieces or ideas to you."

"Let's suppose you had a group of, oh, let's say at least five or six—and ideally, you want to scale that to any number you care to name—of people supplying you with the workforce to get these projects done *and paid for* and you've really got a tidy business going, hmm?"

"The key thing," she emphasised, "is privacy. You mustn't trust others to keep yours and you must respect mine at all times. If we talk on a cell phone, it is only on a cell phone I supply. You're never to come to my home unannounced, and you're never to tell other people where or how to find me."

She handed him an iPhone. "Here's a phone with my private number. You must return this phone when I ask for it. You must not lose it or otherwise dispose of it."

She looked at him sternly. "And there is something else I absolutely insist upon, Alec," she said. "I insist that you never speak of this agreement to others without my express written permission, and I further insist that you never betray my trust or lie to me. Is that something you can promise me?"

Alec solemnly swore to keep his promise.

When the details had all been agreed upon, she presented Alec with a pen and the contract to sign. A moment later, the deal was done.

"I look forward to seeing your proposal outlines and sketches," she said. "Bill will take you back home when you've finished your wine."

"You've been a very good sport listening to all my terms and conditions. Do you have any more questions?" Alec shook his head. "Now," she said, "Come over here. Perhaps I can do something for you."

* * *

When he got home that evening, Alec decided the first thing he needed to do was to see if any of his friends were interested in working on this project with him. The first person he called was Georgia.

The next day, they met at the Old Stag's Head pub and, over a couple of beers, Alec pitched his idea to her. "We need to get a crew together," he said. "We'll get a few people—around six, maybe—as a creative team, and I'll act as the creative director. We'll coproduce some cool new pieces and, who knows, maybe we can sell them through your dad's gallery or whatever."

Georgia agreed that it was an exciting idea. She didn't mention the uncertainty surrounding the gallery, however. Her dad was sick, and the gallery was the least of the family's concerns at the moment.

Georgia contacted some of her art school friends she knew were interested in street art and arranged for Alec to meet them.

"Hi," he said. "Thanks for coming down. My name's Alec. And your name is?"

"My friends call me Mookie."

"What's your specialty, Mookie?"

"Uh, what d' you mean?"

"Sorry, I meant *what kind of artwork* are you best known for?"

"Oh, uh, street art, I guess."

"Yes. Good, thanks."

"And what's your name?"

"My name's Paul, but my mates call me Paulie. You can forget that though, they're all cruel bastards. Nah. I'm kidding ya. Call me Paulie."

"And what's your artistic specialty, Paulie?"

"Well, I've got my piece book here with me. Pretty much anything in there is the stuff I fancy. I like a nice multicolour stencil job, and I'm pretty fast."

"That's great. That's what we like around here too. I'll be in touch."

"And you are?"

"Dal's the name."

"Pleased to meet you Dal. My name's Alec. Tell me, Dal, what's your specialty?"

"My specialty," Dal said slowly, "is being trusty 'n' true, I guess. Prob'ly more that than anything. I'm good at helpin' with stuff. And I'm very reliable."

"Those are all great specialties, thank you," said Alec.

"Hey," said Johnnie, "you're looking for street artists, yeah?"

Alec nodded.

"That's me you're looking for then," Johnnie said, flashing a warm smile. "My specialty is paintin', freehand sprayin', stencils, all that good stuff. You spoke to my mates Paulie and Dal, yeah? We're a pretty good team, we are. You should have all of us. We all go to the art school up the way there. We're practically pros now."

* * *

A year later, the team had officially been christened 'the dreamteam' and Georgia's art-school friends Paul, Johnnie, and Dal were onboard. Paul's new girlfriend Petra had expressed interest in joining but was unimpressed when she discovered that the stencils were all being produced by hand.

"You know, Alec," she said. "There are machines that can cut those stencils directly from your vector artwork. I've used them. Believe me, they're a lot faster—and more accurate, too."

* * *

As appealing as a starting wage of £114,000 a year had sounded to Alec in 2007, even back then he was aware that prices would necessarily follow the immutable rules of supply and demand. There was also the triangle of constraints. When the price is fixed, the scope and/or the resources that can be devoted to a project are necessarily limited.

There was also the simple fact that some of the pieces Alec was offering to Duckie ended up being more popular than others. Naturally, she wanted more of those.

The first thing to go was the limit of ten. Larger editions of some of the most popular pieces were offered as 'studio edition' prints, produced from the original stencils, photo masters or plates. It wasn't long before the economics of the business the Duchess was building were far different than those for the arrangement Alec had originally agreed to.

At one of their many meetings in the back of the Daimler or at her home in Hampstead Heath, Alec challenged her to rethink the fixed monthly budget. His artists, he told her, were increasingly unwilling to work on larger pieces without getting a better deal.

"You have to demonstrate leadership in these matters, Angel," she said. "You must always demonstrate and communicate to them that you have the vision to lead them forward. People are like sheep. They need you to shepherd them through their own feelings of doubt and inadequacy.

They must trust you, but those who do not trust themselves cannot be trusted. You need to lead them to greatness, challenging them to realize their own potential. And that means never giving them reason to doubt you. Do what you must to control them, for you are their manager. Never go back on your word, and never give them a reason to follow someone else. They've chosen you, even more than you have chosen them. So you must rule them justly but firmly. There can be no arguments left unsettled. You are the lawgiver and what you say must be the law. And every law has its consequence for those who cannot abide it. Is that entirely clear to you, Angel?"

"It is," said Alec.

The ideas the crew were coming up with were as varied as their interests and influences, he explained. But many of these proposals simply didn't fit within the budget the way the current deal was structured.

Alec didn't want to wait two more years to move ahead on these plans. £9,500 a month, he argued, would not be enough to stage a major art installation piece—some of the pieces in the Smash Gallery were worth more than that! It would also preclude pieces that required extensive software development or sculptural elements.

"Ideas go pretty cheaply in the arts market, I'm afraid," she replied. "It's all about the execution. It's all in the planning. However," she said, "I understand your concern and I share your enthusiasm for these larger works. I'll tell you what: submit to me a detailed proposal for a larger piece and if I can sell it, we'll come up with a price that makes everybody happy. How's that?"

* * *

Being the object of the Duchess's affection was something of a revelation to Alec, who had until then experienced only the affections of girls close to his own age. He tended to like them a little older but this was something different. Something *muliebre.*

Their tryst after that initial evening of business dealings was the first of many. Other than being absolutely forthright about her sexual tastes and desires, Duckie was never exactly forthcoming about her personal life, but Alec learned that she was a widow, had money, and had very particular ideas of what she wanted to do—and what she wanted done—in bed.

Indeed, it started to seem to Alec like some sort of bizarre art-sex fantasy. She'd pick him up in the Daimler, they'd canoodle in the back seat. He'd bring along a batch of sketches and new ideas from the crew, they'd review them together, and then the clothes would come off.

If the review had gone well—and it usually did—she would approve one or more of the designs for production. She encouraged Alec to pay for even those designs that were *almost* good. Building a library of marketable intellectual property, she said, was the road to prosperity.

And she paid. Decent enough money, thought Alec. Enough to keep him in the pink and then some.

The Duchess knew that Alec and his crew, like so many other young artists, will commit to almost any terrible deal in order get a taste of a better life. And when it tastes like *The Good Life*, they're hooked. It's a sad testament, she thought, to the lack of business prowess of so very many of the otherwise gifted, be they musicians or visual artists.

But she felt good about being able to help these poor individuals, and they certainly helped her. Artists were like raw materials to her, like a resource to be grown and consumed. She had buyers lined up to buy these pieces and the prices had climbed in sync with the rising reputation of the mystery artist she told her customers was known only as TCO.

One might look at such behavior as if she were the Mata Hari of the art brokering world, but, for the most part, the customers didn't object to her terms, and neither did the artists she worked with. She found the ones like Alec, with management potential, and gave them the tools they needed to build out a network of talent. She encouraged them to learn the soft skills of people management and the hard skills of being an art director. Then she put the fruits of their labours in front of the people who knew how to sell them.

One had to be careful not to step on the wrong toes in such matters, but not allowing one's own toes to be stepped on was essential. Being an art broker was, like the product itself, more art than science. It required an understanding of the customers, their expectations, and the optimal paths to reach them. The trick was to understand the relationships the customers had with their preferred auction houses, galleries or, sometimes unavoidably, other brokers. Bypassing the broker was never okay.

Every independent gallery owner she knew, without fail,

was so interested in getting their cut of a big sale, they'd fall into line with her commission-on-sale terms and stipulations. Only the largest and most desirable galleries played by strict rules. And, as it turned out, those were just the sorts of dealers who had top-tier customers. The sort of customers well acquainted with auction-house paddles and protocols.

One of the great advantages of dictating exactly when and where a street art piece would be created had its advantages, chiefly the ability to prepare and provide an easily removable surface upon which the piece would be situated.

The Duchess was quite successful at building a network of people willing to trade opportunities for good money. Sometimes, they'd sell her the right to mount a removable surface on their wall, along with the right to remove it. Those who were being careful in their dealings tried to stick her with the costs and hassles related to getting a city permit for it.

Sometimes she'd get them to sell her a double door or a fascia wall for little more than the cost of providing a better one as a replacement.

And a few—not many—of the really savvy ones realised that street art should stay where it is—that it was at its best where it belonged. And with those people, she would make a deal for street art as a tourist attraction. As the reputation of TCO improved, the street value increased. And if they bought an insurance deal that paid them if it ever disappeared, it usually did. Wash, rinse, repeat.

She never spoke of these things to Alec, or any of the other young men and women she had arrangements with. All they had to do was keep delivering, and keep her name completely out of it.

* * *

Duckie's network of buyers did in fact lead to commissions for ever-larger works. It wasn't long before the ambitions of the team and the cost of the creative studio space Alec rented began to outpace the budget he had earmarked for them. They quickly outgrew the tiny 130 square foot workspace Alec had initially chosen. Alec bought the name Lenz Design from Len, hired Len as a full-time employee and moved to a larger office as soon as the 12-month lease was up.

The new workspace was fully eight times larger than the old hole in the wall. Everybody pitched in to help move into the new space, but it was mostly Alec, Len and Dal who decided where everything should go and moved the equipment into place.

Behind the room with the office at the front of the shop, they set up a large painting surface for banners, a photo-silkscreen and plate-making area, a big cutting board for stencils and frisket masks and desks for computers, scanners and printers. There was even a drive-in area at the back where clients could bring in motorbikes, boats, vans or other vehicles to have them festooned with the studio's unique brand of street art style, which now included proper airbrushing and pinstriping, too.

This was great for everybody—and especially great for Len. His production skills helped improve the quality of the prints and posters they were producing. Alec was out there selling and, by the end of 2010, the work was pouring in. The local bands started placing orders for T-shirts, posters, custom CD covers, and other offset- and screen-printed swag, and soon the shop had a real reputation going as one of the artiest studios in town. They did almost a million pounds worth of work that year—enough that Len was able to step up his game, as he'd long wanted to do, and enough that Alec started approving some of the new investments that Len and the others were suggesting.

His request for a gold-leaf logo for the front door was vetoed ('delayed' was the term Alec used), but his design for an old-style hanging sign was approved—and it looked great with its wrought-iron bracket and elegant *Garamond* typeface.

They set up an area of the front office as a store, with bins full of prints and posters offered for sale.

To his credit, Alec was quite forthright with the crew about the fact that their designs were being sold to galleries as prints or other media. The creator of the piece got paid for the original approved design and for each and every one of the original limited-edition prints. And Alec was quite successful at convincing them all to allow their work to be attributed to the mythical persona of TCO.

It wasn't hard, really. TCO was becoming a *bona fide* phenomenon. As prices for pieces signed by "TCO" at auction houses and on gallery walls steadily increased, the art-world media had plenty to say about the mysterious unknown artist. They speculated on his or her identity, just as they'd speculated about the identity of Banksy a decade earlier. TCO followers and arts media reporters gathered at the location of the latest piece to take photographs and speculate on its implications.

The dreamteam, of course, never mentioned their connection to this towering mythical figure. They knew that their pieces were being reattributed to TCO and sold to an eager marketplace for far more than their own reputations could command. Alec had convinced them that when the time came that the TCO persona was retired, their reputations as top-tier artists and, indeed, mythmakers was all but guaranteed. Until then, they just had to play the game, keep the secret, and keep producing. And Alec, now working more closely with Len, would ensure that the production quality and the design consistency kept improving.

They also decided it would be prudent to develop an emergency plan. Georgia had posed the question initially: what will we do if we are caught in the act of producing a TCO piece?

Alec said, "First rule: we must never preannounce or attribute a piece before it is completed. That way, we can simply deny that it is by TCO.

Len offered a second suggestion, which he read from a piece of paper: "If it is argued that any person or persons on the team are involved with activities attributed to TCO, we should, without undue delay, have other members of the group act secretly in such a way as to show that the accused party could *not* be TCO, by posting and attributing a piece of evidence prepared in such a way that it clears the accused's name by providing apparent proof of their non-involvement."

"Man, you sound like a lawyer," said Dal.

Alec interjected: "You should destroy that piece of paper right now. Rule number two: no physical evidence of any involvement with, or direct relationship to, TCO. That means no mentions of any non-public TCO information in any form. No emails, no little notes, no phone messages, nothing. I will handle all external communication and, if I am unable to do that, one person and one person only should handle that task. Any questions?"

Petra added: "But we're all committed to helping one another, if we do get into a jam, aren't we?"

"Yes. Yes, of course."

Alec reiterated what he claimed was the whole point of this charade: by building a brand name for their work that provided both anonymity and notoriety, he was able to sell the work on the market and ensure that everyone got paid. And, although he left out the part where it wasn't actually him doing the selling, it was all above board.

And aside from Petra, who declined to submit most of her best work, they all said they were happy to be making an average of 500 pounds per piece. It was roughly 500 more than they would otherwise be making for doing what they loved to do—and certainly not a bad wage for a few hours' work.

However, Paul, Petra and Georgia were more vocal about their dissatisfaction with the pay for the higher-risk wall jobs. Alec acknowledged their concerns and promised them he'd try to figure out how to make it more worthwhile for everyone. *Boy, the days of painting for pizzas and beer are long gone,* he thought.

Petra sometimes wondered why she was allowed to be

a part of the crew, despite her limited participation. Paul's theory was in fact correct: Alec valued her artistic opinion enough that she was the *de facto* arbiter of style for the team. She had an impeccable sense of what was or wasn't *good* and she wasn't shy about making her opinion known.

Indeed, Alec's Tuesday night meetings gave him a chance to hear the opinions and draw together the unique areas of expertise of all the members of the team. Each person had a unique skill set. Len brought production expertise and typographic skills. Georgia knew her art history and the gallery scene. Paul had oodles of raw talent. Johnnie brought the wit, and Dal was as trusty as he'd promised he would be. And there was Petra, with her impeccable taste.

An Invitation

Alec's mother stood outside his bedroom door at 10:00 a.m. "The schoolmaster sent another copy of your school marks," she said in that annoying voice she used when she was displeased, which seemed to be all the time these days. "You know, after the first ones went missing."

"Shit," Alec whispered to himself, as he put down his marker. He was working on an updated version of his tag, and he didn't like to be interrupted while he worked. Still, he thought, it was coming along nicely. The letter A just needed a bit more … something.

"Your dad and I have had a look and we're very disappointed that you're not keepin' up, son. It's a requirement, Allie."

"Yeah, I know mum," said Alec, trying hard not to sound as bored as he was of this topic.

"You've got an incomplete score in your GCSEs and not been going to your A-levels, they tell me. This simply won't do."

"But I don't care about A-Levels, mum. I'm an artist. That's all I care about."

"An artist? What, selling your drawings? You think you're going to make a decent living doing that? You've not even been to a proper art school."

"I'm already making a decent living at it, mum. I've got people who believe in me. And *I* believe in me. You've got to have a dream, don't you, mum?"

"I'm not going to be drawn into a philosophical argument about this with you, Allie," she sighed. "You know, if you got your A-levels sorted out, you could be an art teacher or something that gives you some career certainty. Some job prospects, you know."

"I don't give a rat's arse about any of that."

"Well, you'll have to talk more about your schooling with your father. He's very upset with you right now, so you'd best tread lightly if you don't want to be out on your ear. And don't go avoiding him. He's ticked, I'm tellin' you. An' don't be goin' on about your dreams with him, either. You'd do all right if you were as practical as he is," she said loudly from the hall as his bedroom door clicked shut.

Alec sat at his desk and opened the top drawer. From it, he pulled a manila folder and a black binder. He opened the 3-ring binder clips and, from the back of the binder, he retrieved a small stack of empty plastic page protectors. Into each of these 3-hole plastic page protectors, he inserted a black matte background and onto each side of that, he slid a drawing or photo. When he was done, he pressed the clips closed again and reviewed his new additions. As he paged through the new items, he decided that the order could be improved. He clicked the binder clips open again and rearranged two of the new pages. One last click and he was done. He returned the manila folder to the drawer and pulled out his phone. *Great news,* he texted. *New project ideas ready to show.*

Alec closed his binder and slipped it into his backpack. He tied the laces of his new shoes and stepped out into the late morning sun. Today, though, there wasn't a car waiting. Today he didn't need help from Dal or anyone else. He just needed to get into his dad's workshop. And get the keys for his truck.

* * *

Len's phone buzzed as he was walking down Build Lane with a vinyl copy of the debut album by *Children of Angels* under his arm. It was Tuesday afternoon and Alec and the crew were scheduled to get together at 8 o'clock as usual at the Old Stag's Head pub on Holywell.

Another text arrived a few seconds later. *Can u make it?*

Len checked the time and sent a *Y.*

Just north of Shoreditch station, Len was stopped in his

tracks by a sight so comedic and so awful, he couldn't believe his eyes. There, pasted onto the plywood wall of yet another construction site, was a Frankenstein's monster version of his Moloko poster, horribly redrawn, with off-centred and overcrowded headlines, muddy colours and crude halftones. Skewed text instead of proper italics. And printed on crap paper to boot. It was a hack job through and through. It was for a different event at the club but this abomination was clearly based on his design. He looked at the fine print in the border and there it was: credited to Mack Designs. Fuck you Bob.

* * *

By the time Len arrived at the Old Stag's Head public house on Holywell Row, Dal, Georgia, and Alec were already there. As usual, Alec had reserved the table at the back for them. Unexpectedly, Danielle was there with him. Len wondered: was *she* going to join the crew? And a couple of minutes after 8 pm, Paul, Petra, and Johnnie arrived and apologised for being late.

"Some of you have already met Danielle. She's here tonight because I wanted to show you all something a little bit special I've been working on."

Alec moved the stack of menus that covered the middle of the table. When the others saw what was underneath them, it was clear that Alec had indeed prepared something special for tonight's meeting. Len's face lit up with a big smile. Petra tugged on Paul's sleeve and directed his attention to what was going on at the table.

"Oo-wee," said Paul. "Aren't we the fancy ones?"

The centre of the rectangular table now had Len's dreamteam logo—with a bright and beautiful woodgrain texture!—underneath its varnished surface. The team now had its very own customised table and of course, being an ambigram, you could read it from either side of the table.

Alec buffed the surface with his serviette. "Isn't it beautiful?"

The others crowded around for a closer look. "That's fockin' epic," said Johnnie. "'How'd you manage that, Alec?" Alec just shrugged and flashed that enigmatic smile.

In fact, it had been quite a lot of work. But helping his dad with woodworking projects was something that Alec had always enjoyed as a kid. His dad had shown him how to cut table tops to size (measure twice, cut once!) smooth the edges and carve designs with a router, then pour polyurethane and blow off the bubbles to get a perfectly smooth surface. And that's what he'd done here. Underneath the smooth polyurethane surface of the table, the logo had been carefully routed into the stained wood. And so here it was, the dreamteam logo, immortalised on their very own handcrafted table. Not even Dal had seen the table before tonight. Alec and his dad had finished it, assembled it, and delivered it themselves. Len felt really special to be sitting there.

And that wasn't even the highlight of the evening for Len. When he headed off to the washroom, he was intercepted outside the men's room door by Danielle, who slipped him a piece of paper. "Call me," she whispered discreetly.

When he returned from the men's room, Len's mood had improved enough that Georgia wondered if there was a washroom party she hadn't been invited to. "Hey Georgia," he said, "I've been meaning to ask you: have you ever had any neon work done at that custom neon place that's just down the street a bit?"

"The one on Holywell?"

"Yes, right around the corner."

"Yeah, sort of," she said. "My neon guy used to work with them. He bends his own neon now, so we don't use them anymore. I hope you get a chance to meet our guy. He goes by the name 'After Midnight' and he's a real character. Drives a big convertible. Good neon bender, too."

She motioned for him to sit across from her.

"One of the things he told me about working there was quite interesting. He says he worked there as an apprentice bender for more than two years with an older guy named Bracey and he never knew that this old guy was a living legend in the neon business. He'd personally done many of the most famous neon pieces in London. You know, the really big pieces in Piccadilly Circus and all around Soho and elsewhere around town, back when everyone was trying to outdo each other in having the most neon. He was one of the greats and my guy said he never bragged about any of it or even mentioned them when he was working there. Bracey was always looking ahead."

She picked at the corner of her coaster absent-mindedly. "Anyway, so our guy learned the trade from one of the greats."Len asked: "I notice you often use the word 'our' when you're talking about the gallery. Do you have partners?"

She laughed ruefully and said: "No, not really, unless you consider the bank a partner. My ex-husband used to be a partner, but he's out of the picture now. Thank goodness."

"I guess it's the fact that most of the neon in the gallery is by 'After Midnight,' that I think of it as 'our' stuff. But I'm the owner, and I give him a place to sell his works in exchange for a cut of the profits. It's not that different than the arrangements we have with other artists, other than the fact that we kind of specialise in neon a bit."

"You're not saying that 'After Midnight' is your ex-husband, are you?"

"Oh God no, my ex had no artistic talent whatsoever. His only talent was in talking wealthy people into buying very expensive pieces of artwork. Until he decided he didn't want to do that. Long story, not really worth going into."

"Well I appreciate your candor," said Len. "It's very refreshing."

Georgia didn't mention it, but her father had actually been the original owner of the gallery. It had a different name then, and when he passed on, the gallery had been bequeathed to her. Her former husband's involvement had simply been a bad decision made when she was very young.

* * *

"For our next project, I want us to produce something on the theme of social responsibility," Alec announced. "I want us to produce something that really sets us apart from the very average crowd out there—something that sets a high bar for quality and also sets us apart in terms of social awareness. I want our upcoming pieces to be the best pieces in the neighbourhood. I'm looking for something that provides context for taking action in the form of dissent, social activism, protests against police brutality, and that sort of thing. And, as it's a wall job and I promised I'd look into how to further incentivise those, I'm going to pay double the usual rate." *God, I sound like a businessman*, he thought.

Alec had heard about the rumblings of discontent about the pay for the last job—mostly from Paul and Georgia, both of whom had declined to participate—and he was trying to restore a positive sentiment of his crew. And doubling the pay seemed like a good place to start. Besides, Alec knew enough about Georgia's situation to understand that she wasn't really in the position to be turning down extra income when it became available.

"Are you thinking along the lines of opposing bland corporatism, or something stronger?" Petra asked.

"I definitely want it to be a provocative message. And based on an evocative image."

"In case you need some ideas to work with," he said, "I've

pulled some recent clips of police brutality and race riots in clips from America and around the world." Alec said the images, many of which were of the Oakland riots following the killing of Oscar Grant by a BART police officer, were "fresh from the news." He challenged the crew to "recontextualize" the violent imagery into something that creates a positive message of hope, an opportunity for change, or a chance for justice. That was the thing about Alec. He always tried to *act* like a leader.

"We'll have to doctor the images to avoid being accused of copyright infringement," Paul warned.

Alec looked skeptical. "Really?" he asked. "I was thinking more along the lines of Mickey Mouse throwing the fockin' teargas. Or, I dunno, maybe somebody throwing it *at* him. He could be wearing SWAT gear or something."

Dal looked at it thoughtfully for a moment and said, "It kinda works both ways."

"I'd prefer to avoid any overtly violent imagery," said Johnnie. "There's more than enough violence out there already. We can be socially relevant without being shocking."

"It can be anything you want," Alec assured him. "Go with animal rights if you want to. Just come up with a powerful concept and bring to the meeting next week. Just try to make an important statement."

Len reached into his backpack. "Hey Alec," he said. "I have been working on another idea that I think might interest you." He pulled out a handful of wooden sticks connected with string. "This is a scale model," he explained. "But watch this." He lifted the two end pieces up and the other parts fell into the shape of a box. He swung the dangling side pieces up into position as cross braces and secured them with the attached velcro fasteners.

A few seconds later, he stood the now-stable frame on the table and slid a piece of cardboard into the bottom section. "This would be something strong enough to stand on, of course," he explained. "And we'd probably use zip ties instead of velcro for extra strength. But it's quite strong and it's really lightweight. And quiet while it's going up, too."

"Bravo," said Alec. "That looks quite promising. I guess we have to build a bigger one and see if it works, eh?" *Now I'm paying double for wall jobs and funding R&D, as well,* he thought.

"Now we just need one of those gizmos that shoots a hook and a cable into the ceiling of a building and we won't need the ladders at all," said Paul, only half-joking.

"We'll have to build a full-size prototype and make sure it's safe, of course," said Len,

"but I think it should be. I did a bit of research about how they build scaffolds like this in Hong Kong and elsewhere."

"Apparently, they've got quite a state-of-the-art scaffold system over there at Buckingham Palace," said Petra.

"Yeah, I read about that one, too. They patented that system. Really strong and safe."

"Well, no doubt. You'll upgrade us to that one next time, eh, Alec?" Paul joked.

"Not designed for speedy or quiet assembly, though."

"Here's to Len," said Alec, raising his glass. The others raised theirs. "Well done."

The next day, Alec gave Len £500 cash toward the purchase of the structural materials, tarps and pulley systems they'd need to build a prototype of Len's experimental scaffolding system. He knew it would be more, but this was all he could afford at the moment.

* * *

The following Tuesday, Georgia was perched on a small aluminum stepladder, adjusting the lighting in the presentation room to best show off the picture a client was coming in to view, when the door chime sounded. She poked her head around the corner. It was Len.

"Hello up there," he said. "I just came down to see the gallery, and maybe take you out for coffee—or tea?"

"Oh, I can't get away today," she said. "I'm the only one here on Tuesdays."

Len followed her black stockings up toward the lights she was working on. "Can I grab a sandwich for you, maybe? Or a muffin or something?"

"It's very kind of you to offer, but really, I've got a lunch here I haven't had time to eat yet." She climbed down from the ladder and tugged on the arm of his jacket. "Hey," she said, "come and look at your poster. I've got one in a frame here." She pulled him over to the wall on the exterior side of the presentation room, and there it was: his signed poster, in a gleaming black frame. "That's non-glare, UV-resistant glass there," she pointed out. "And that matte border complements it quite nicely, doncha think?"

"Yeah, really nice job on that," said Len. The matte

certainly made the poster look larger. He looked at the price. *Jeez.* £250. At least his name was on the tag.

"They've been selling quite well," said Georgia. "It's a great design."

She moved the stepladder aside and pointed toward the back of the gallery. "Please take a look around. There's lots of stuff I think you'll like. We've got a whole neon art section on that back wall, and a few more up in the front. In fact, that's how the gallery got started—hence, the name."

"Yeah, I like that one in the window. Is it a flying spaghetti monster?"

"It sure is. The one and only."

"I think it's fantastic."

"Well, not everyone does, but I like it too."

"Fortunately, the people most likely to be offended are also the ones least likely to know what it symbolises."

"I commissioned it from After Midnight," she explained, "after I tried to interest Alec in doing something—anything —with it. It's called *Ego pascat te.*"

She wanted to tell Len how annoyed she was with Alec sometimes, when she'd bring him a good idea and he'd say "Bravo" or something like that and then... nothing. He'd do absolutely nothing with the idea. Georgia preferred a more iterative approach to creativity. Doing the Flying Spaghetti

Monster up in glorious neon wasn't the only way to bring it to life.

Len turned to look at the other neon pieces along the back wall.

"Anyway," Georgia said, "have a look around, and don't hesitate to ask, if you've got any questions."

"Don't mind me," she said, as she returned to the presentation room. "I've got to get this lighting set up before 3 pm."

"So, what time are you off? We could go out for a bite to eat or something…" he suggested.

"Gee, I don't think so, sorry Len," she said. Len was just a bit too *industrial*, she'd decided. She preferred men with smoother hands.

"Hey, I do have one question," he said. "Do you know where Alec lives?"

"Funny you should ask that," said Georgia. "Petra and I were just wondering about that the other day. I don't know, but you might want to ask her."

Georgia thought back to 2007—it seemed so long ago!—when she and Alec were dating. The fact that she never got to know where he lived was a problem *then*, too. He was a frequent visitor to the gallery back in those days and her friend After Midnight used to invite them both out to go cruising with him in his wonderful old pearl-white 1960 Cadillac convertible, with its lovely whitewall tyres and those crazy tail fins. She never once saw that car with the top up. It always seemed like summer in that back seat, as the tape deck blasted out the soundtrack of their youth. They'd be bouncing around there in the back, laughing and singing, on that huge sofa-sized back seat. After Midnight, who had come from Canada, used to call it 'the chesterfield.' Those were such good times. Back when After Midnight was still going out with Petra. Before Paul was part of the scene; before her younger self met Mr. Wrong. Before the arguments with Alec began. Before the crew even existed.

She realised Len was talking. "...I managed to get a look at the registration papers for the van and I made a note of the address, so we should be able to locate Alec that way," he said. "I figure that's easier and safer than trying to follow him home after a meeting, you know?"

"So you have his address? Well done, Len," she said. "You're quite a sleuth." She was amazed that he could discover a piece of information in a few days that she'd been after for *years.*

Len knew she must be curious—and he needed a ride. "I was wondering if perhaps you'd like to take a drive up there with me to, you know, do a bit of sleuthing?"

"Yes, that sounds promising," she said.

"You mentioned that Petra had expressed interest as well; do you think we should invite her along?"

"She'd probably like that. I think she's even more curious than I am. I'll ask." She dialed Petra's phone number. "Hey Petra. Yeah, hi. Len thinks he might have come across Alec's home address, and we're going to drive up there to take a look. Interested in coming along?"

"Uh, I don't think so," said Petra. It would be terribly embarrassing to be caught snooping around, she thought. "But thanks anyway and, by all means, let me know what you discover. 'Be invisible,' as Alec would say."

Seven

Riddles and Stories

A text message from Georgia arrived on Len's phone just after 10:30 the next morning. "Are you ready for our little adventure?" it said.

"Ready now," he replied.

"Text me your address and I'll pick you up in 10 minutes."

Ten minutes later, a silver 1986 BMW M5 series saloon pulled up outside Len's flat where he was waiting. The sidewalk-side window opened and Petra leaned into view. "Get in," she said tersely.

"Cool car," said Len. It was nice of him to say that, she thought, but she knew it was getting a little long in the tooth. Nevertheless, the E28 had more cachet with collectors than any new car she could reasonably afford.

After a quick pit stop for coffees at the local café, they headed off on their quest.

"It's east of Regent's Park," Len said as he looked at the map on his phone.

"Hmm, nice neighbourhood," said Georgia. Maybe Alec was on the level after all.

"That's it," said Alec as they arrived at the address on Prince Albert Road.

"My, my," said Georgia. "Very posh." They slowed down as they drove past. On the other side of a hedge was a gated driveway.

Just outside the garage door was the Bentley, surrounded by the damp signs of a recent carwash. "Hey, that's the car, isn't it?"

"That's it, all right," said Len. "Pull over. There."

As they watched from the far side of the street, the garage door opened up and out of the shadows strode Dal, a polishing cloth in hand. He wiped the side mirrors and the front windshield. On the other side of the garage was the white van. The front door of the house opened and a woman emerged from the shadows inside.

In a hushed voice—but still too loud!—Len said, "Look—there's a woman coming...."

"Shhh," Georgia whispered as the woman's voice called out.

"Dallas! Lunch is ready."

"I think that's his mom," Georgia whispered.

"Dallas?" said Len. "I never thought of him as a 'Dallas.'"

They realised this was Dal's house, not Alec's.

Len was suddenly nervous. "If Dal sees us, he'll blab for sure," he said, turning away. "Let's get out of here."

"I can't really afford to hang around all afternoon waiting

for him to leave," said Georgia, starting the car. "I've got things to do."

"Maybe we could follow them *after* the meeting tonight," Len suggested.

Georgia thought for a moment, then put the car into gear and pulled onto the road. "I dunno," she said. "Seems awfully risky to me. It's pretty obvious when you're being followed by a car."

"Oh, I'm sure we could manage it, if we keep our distance and don't look too obvious. Have you got a hat or something you can wear to provide a bit of a disguise?"

Georgia shook her head and looked unimpressed. "You seem to be a bit more invested in this than me, Len," she said. "I mean, I'm curious and all, but isn't this a bit obsessive?" She had been accused of stalking her ex back when he was cheating on her, and *that* whole episode lingered in her memory like a bad smell in the air. Not to mention the fact that Alec would almost certainly get the wrong idea if *he* discovered her snooping around.

"I am investigating this for one simple reason," said Len. "I'm a big believer in the old saying: 'follow the money.' I've been keeping track of the money Alec's been spending on our projects, at the clubs and pubs, on fancy restaurants, girl-friends, cars, equipment, custom tables, personalised hoodies, and so on and honestly, there's an awful lot of money being spent. And that's only the stuff I've personally seen. Who knows how much else is being spent? Where's all this money coming from?"

"Mummy and daddy?" suggested Georgia.

"Maybe. He's either very rich or there's something else going on that we don't know about. And if he's a big-time dope dealer or something, we might be at risk of being flagged as accomplices. I mean, I like what I see. It's what I *don't* see that worries me."

"You used to go out with him, didn't you?" he asked. "Was he always this extravagant?"

Georgia shook her head. "No, you're right. He never used to be this way. I never really thought about it. There's so much wining and dining in the art world, I kind of thought he was just stepping up his game—becoming more of a player, if you know what I mean."

Len knew all too well what she meant. And he took that as an admission of why Georgia had turned him down. As he looked at the rings on her fingers, he said, "He asked me not to disclose this, but he pays me money, you know. For designs. So what's that all about?"

Len was deliberately a bit vague with Georgia on this point, as he wasn't sure if anyone else on the crew was getting a wage, as he was.

"Yeah," said Georgia. "He pays me, and I think he pays Dal, Johnnie and Paul, too. Petra's the only one, I think, who's decided not to sell stuff to him. But she told me she used to. In fact, that's kinda how we got onto this topic in the first place."

"There are other things I've been wondering about, too," Len said. "Alec comes to us with ideas for themes, but you've probably noticed he *always* takes a few days to decide on which theme to go with, as if there's some external decision or approval that's required. So when I add it all up, it really starts to look like there's more to this picture than what we're seeing," he said. "I want to know what's going on, just for my own peace of mind. Besides, we're not breaking any laws."

Georgia shook her head. "Well, I still don't want him to have any reason to suspect that he's being followed. And he *did* tell us all how important it is to 'be invisible.' I know I wouldn't like it if *I* learned that someone was sneaking around watching what I was doing."

"I'll make sure that doesn't happen," Len assured her. "I could drive next time if you want," he offered.

"*Next* time? You don't give up easily, do you?" *Points for tenacity*, she thought.

"Give up? No way. I *know* we're close to the answer. We already know that Dal drives Alec around in that Bentley, and we already know where Alec gets driven to every Tuesday night. It's not that much of a trick to follow him back home one of these Tuesday nights."

"So remind me why we're running around out here now, then?"

Len couldn't quite tell if there was an edge of hostility in her voice. "Please. I had an address, I thought it was his address. Look, I'll pay for the gas and I'll drive next time, OK?"

"You've got a license?"

"Yeah. I just don't have a car."

"Well, I'm willing to give it one last try," said Georgia. "If you think you can do it without being spotted, let's give it a go after the meeting. Or ... on second thought, do you think that following Dal from his house to wherever he picks up Alec might be easier?"

"No, I thought about that. I think it's quite a bit riskier. For one thing, your car would be much easier to identify before the sun goes down and secondly, Alec is much less likely to be home earlier in the evening. You know, he might be out having dinner or whatever."

"Yeah," Georgia decided, "I guess the risk is higher. Okay. We'll follow them afterwards."

"We'll have to know where the car is parked, though," said Len, in full planning mode.

"I'll stay outside and watch for them when they arrive."

"Shouldn't be too hard. There aren't that many places to hide a car around that pub. And if they see you, just make out like you've just arrived, too."

"Yeah, perfect."

The following Tuesday at 7:55 p.m., Georgia was watching from an alcove on the far side of the street as the Bentley pulled up outside the pub on the corner and Alec exited the car and entered the pub. She watched as Dal drove off down Holywell and turned right. She ran across the street to see if he was coming up the road on the other side. Fortunately, she saw the car backing into a parking spot near the middle of the block. "Parked" she texted Len as she stepped into the pub.

At 7:58 p.m., Dal joined the group as a round of beers arrived at the table. At 8 p.m. sharp, the meeting was brought to order.

"I hope everyone brought their 'social responsibility' ideas," said Alec. "Who wants to start?"

Paul and Johnnie showed a design they'd both worked on. It was brilliant, albeit fiendishly complex. It was an all-black Disney cartoon family, living in squalor in a rundown Toon-town ghetto. "Johnnie did a lot of work on this," said Paul, "so credit where credit's due."

"Thanks, mate," said Johnnie.

As he had suggested he might, Alec went with a dark Disney theme: A gunsight crosshair aimed at Mickey's head.

"Did I misunderstand the assignment? I didn't do Disney," said Len with a wink. His contribution was a spoof of the Clash's *London Calling* album art, entitled *London Crawling 'Traffic Clash,'* featuring a figure in a pose resembling the one on the original cover. But instead of smashing a guitar, the figure is hanging on to a parking meter, as if desperately trying to insert the required change before the meter runs out.

The meter-pole itself has been pushed off-centre, as if it has been damaged, and coins litter the ground.

"Ha ha. I love that album," said Dal.

"Nice. And not too complicated to pull off in a few hours," said Alec, in what seemed to Paul and Johnnie like a backhanded way of implying that their piece *was.*

"I know that there aren't any meters that look quite like that anymore—I hope that doesn't look like an error. Having coins spilled out of a derelict parking meter that looks like it's been knocked over a bit is intentional."

"An error? It's *a nuclear error*, Len!" said Johnnie with a wink.

"Oh my goodness, this one is really something," said Georgia, when she saw Petra's offering.

Petra's piece was a riff on the imagery of American Gothic, except in this version, a grayscale photorealistic depiction of the couple wearing gasmasks showed them standing next to the painting that made them famous.

"I call it *American Gothic Horror*," she said.

Alec studied it with admiration. "Fantastic. Pretty complicated to paint on a wall, though."

Georgia suggested that, if they really wanted to be daring and provocative, they should do a self-portrait of TCO. "I was looking at this book of stuff by René Magritte," she said. And there is this piece of his called *The Great War*, ostensibly a self-portrait of the artist wearing a bowler hat, but the artist's face is completely obscured by an apple. I thought it might be fun if we did a similar piece, but with a spraycan or a big paintbrush or something covering the artist's face."

Provocative indeed. That's probably the one that would get the most press, the others agreed. Alec didn't seem sold on the idea, though, probably because they nominated him as the one to wear the bowler hat.

"Bravo everyone," said Alec.

Georgia leaned close to Petra. "Can you come to the ladies room with me?" Georgia asked her.

Petra nodded and finished her beer.

Inside the washroom, Georgia asked her: "Did you bring a car?"

"No, I came with Paul," she said.

"Can you make some sort of excuse to come with us when the meeting's over?" she asked. "And we can talk then."

"I think I can manage that," said Petra.

The meeting adjourned a little earlier than usual and, as planned, Georgia offered to give Petra a ride home and she and Len stood outside the pub as they waited for Petra to come out.

"I've decided to drive after all," whispered Georgia to Len. "If we do get spotted, I just can't imagine explaining why you'd be driving my car. One beer is not much of an excuse to have a designated driver, especially if I've just offered to drive Petra home. It just wouldn't make sense."

"No worries," said Len. "We'll be fine. We're invisible."

"Here she comes," said Georgia as Petra stepped off the curb and headed toward them.

"Being on the east side of the area where Dal parked, the car should be easy to spot as it passes by the corner," Georgia reasoned. "We are well positioned to be able to follow Dal as soon as he and Alec leave, no matter which way he turns."

A moment later, they all sat in the car waiting. The Bentley drove past the corner, just as they'd expected. "There it goes."

Georgia pulled the BMW out of its spot and waited until the Bentley was a half-block ahead before turning to follow it.

"So you went out to that address today?" Petra asked them as the car picked up speed. "Did you find out anything interesting?"

"Well, we found out where Dal lives," said Georgia. "The car and the van are *his*."

"Hmm. That's something, I guess."

"A bit of a letdown, really," admitted Len.

She nodded. "But Dal will drop Alec off after the meeting, yeah?"

"That's the plan. The theory is that Dal must know where Alec lives, given that he picks him up in his car all the time. Len figures if we follow Dal's car tonight, we'll learn where he drops Alec off."

"Hm, yes. Sounds like it might work."

"Anything else?"

"Well, it looks like the company name on the van's registration must be some sort of shell corporation that Dal's family uses. We're pretty sure Alec doesn't live at Dal's place."

"Dal's in a very nice neighbourhood, by the way. Up by Regent's Park."

"The Regents Park. Oh darlings. Mummy and daddy must be sitting pretty."

"Positively tweedy."

"Hey," said Len, as they passed a billboard. "What about re-subvertising one of the big political campaign billboards as a spoof of an NHS billboard advertising a remedy for those 'suffering from affluenza?'"

"Yeah, 'Wash your hands more often... of responsibility'—I like it," said Petra.

"That's pretty good. We should suggest it."

"OK, I'll work on it," said Len.

They followed Dal's car north and east toward the fringe of central London, to the borough of Islington near the canal called Angel.

The car turned at the sign for the Regent's Canal and parked near the tunnel.

Petra pointed to an open gate. "I think this path leads to the canal. There are houseboats down there."

No wonder he never took me to his house when we were going out, thought Georgia.

"There he is. He's climbing onto that boat down there. It's the second one from the end."

"Can you still see him?"

"No."

"Let's get a little closer."

They heard a woman's voice. "I think that might be Danielle," said Petra.

"I don' believe you," shouted the woman with a French accent. It was definitely Danielle.

As the three of them watched from the stairwell to the walkway, they heard an increasingly loud argument.

"I can't listen to this," said Georgia, who appeared visibly distraught by the sounds of a doomed relationship. She began backing away from the others. "Trust me, she'll be kicking him out of there any second now. We should get the hell out of here."

Sure enough, a moment later, the shouting match was over and Alec, jacket in hand, emerged from the cabin and clambered back onto the walkway. The sound of the slamming cabin door said it all.

Alec glanced back at the boat, then pulled out his cellphone and began texting as he walked.

"Shit. He's coming this way. Let's go—quickly."

Back in the car, Georgia said, "I don't think that was Alec's place either."

"Yeah," said Petra. "It sounded like that was *her* place. I think I'm done with this."

Len had been worrying that the number Danielle had given him was some sort of trap. That suddenly seemed far less likely. Now, he was worried that he'd wasted too much time on these wild goose chases to have any credibility left. But Alec had already disappeared up the walkway. For now, at least, it was a moot point.

* * *

Len was in the kitchen buttering a piece of toast when there was a *knock-knock-knock* on the door. He opened it and was surprised to see Danielle standing there.

"Oh, thank goodness. I knocked on two other doors. Those poor people didn't know you. You should make friends with your neighbours, I think." She smiled.

"You're absolutely right. I definitely should. But what a surprise. What brings you to my neighbourhood?"

"May I come in?" she asked.

"Of course, my apologies. How rude of me. I also want to apologise for not calling you back yet. I've been very busy."

"*Non*, it's fine. I don't invite myself into people's homes very often, you know. But I really wanted to talk to you about what happened the other night."

Len wondered what she meant. Did she somehow learn that he'd overheard the shouting match on the boat?

"What do you know about that girl Zena we went out with?" she asked him.

"Honestly, practically nothing. I think she said she was a friend of Alec's... or was she a friend of yours?"

"So, you didn't know her? Please don't lie to me," she pleaded.

"I would never..."

"You remember when the three of us went out?"

"Yes, of course."

"She and I went to the washroom, you know. And do you know what she said to me?"

Len shook his head. "Would you like tea?"

"No, she asked me if I was an escort. You know, like a hooker."

"What...?"

"And of course, I told her, no I'm not. I'm just a friend."

"What a weird thing for her to say," mused Len.

"So, you know, I was very confused by that. So, I asked

her why she asked me a question like that. And do you know what she said?"

"I can't imagine," said Len.

"She said she 'really shouldn't say.' Like she was *not supposed to tell me*. So of course, it makes me wonder. What's going on?"

"Hmm. I have to think about that for a moment." Len got up and looked at his cold toast still sitting on the counter. He pushed it aside and lifted the teapot to judge its weight instead. "Pardon me," he said, "would you like a cup of tea?"

"Me? Yes, that would be nice. Just black, no milk or sugar, please."

"So," Len said as he poured two cups and handed one to Danielle, "it sounds to me like she didn't really know Alec all that well."

"I know. That's what I thought. And she was very pretty. And so, I asked him, why is he picking up other women if he's supposed to be going out with me? You know, it's not like we were really going steady or anything, but still, it was surprising to me. And I didn't like being asked if I am a hooker."

"Of course."

Suddenly, Alec's obsession with looking like a big shot all seemed to make sense. The charade served multiple purposes: to instill a bit of insecurity that would keep Danielle feeling the need to be competitive, but most of all, to put on a show of affluence that made Alec look powerful and important. That was the reason Alec's efforts to acquire designs and rights from the others at bargain prices were so successful. We'd all seen the power and *we wanted it.*

"Mmm, the tea is good, she said. "So, why do you think Alec invited her?"

"I don't know—to impress me, maybe? It's not really my place to say..." said Len.

"*Au contraire*," she said. "I think you know him better than I do."

"Well, not much, perhaps, but still... I think he should have told you upfront about what was going on."

"Yes!" she said emphatically.

"Nobody likes to be blindsided."

"Sorry, my English is not too good; I don't know that word," said Danielle. "What is 'blindsided'?"

"My apologies," he said. "That is not a very common word, is it? It means 'to be caught unprepared'—in other words, surprised by an unexpected attack."

"Ah, yes, of course. Nobody likes that. You know, I think you are correct. Alec is always trying to impress everyone with his fancy car and fancy restaurants, hey? He had that guy with the big car drive me home that night from the big art show, you know? Like a real big shot. So, bringing along a fancy looking woman to impress you is not such a surprise."

"That was a very good restaurant, wasn't it?"

A look of realisation flickered across Danielle's face. Alec and Zena were probably in the washroom together. "Did she, you know, fool around with either of you guys?"

"What?—ha ha! Not with me. It's funny, you know, I was going to ask Alec if he knew how I could get in touch with her again."

"You liked her, eh?"

"Well, we had a nice time…. I guess it will be interesting to hear what Alec says if I ask him how to get in touch with her. I'll ask him how I can reach her."

"He'll have some sort of excuse. He always does. We had a big argument, you know."

Len pretended to be surprised. "Really?"

"Yes, I don't think he's a good person in his heart. He doesn't care about my feelings."

"Well, I'm very sorry to hear that. You deserve better. More tea?"

"No, thank you. I really should be going. You have been a big help to me. As a way of thanking you, could I buy you a drink or something? Maybe we could meet at the Hoxton Hotel? I stayed there for a couple of days, so I know it's quite nice. Maybe tomorrow?"

"I'd like that. Tomorrow would be just fine. How's 1 o'clock?"

"Maybe 2 o'clock would be better for me," she smiled. "I'll meet you on the patio, okay?"

"I'm looking forward to it. See you then."

Eight

The Duchess

When Len arrived at the Hoxton Hotel café at the agreed-upon time, Danielle was already there, looking very *Parisienne* in her sunglasses and a wide-brimmed hat at a table for two outside on the patio. "Is this shady enough for you?" she asked.

"Oh it's perfect," said Len. "Can I buy you a drink?" he asked.

She smiled and said: "Let me buy you one. What will you have?"

He looked at her bright red drink. "Oh, I don't know. What's that you're drinking?"

"Oh, this is something I acquired a taste for when I went to Italy. You know that the drinking age there is only 16? It's called Campari. I used to drink it with orange juice, but now I like it with ice and a bit of soda. It's kind of an acquired taste. You probably wouldn't like it. You want to try a taste?" She offered him her glass. "I warn you, it's takes a little getting used to."

"It's always fun to try something new," he said confidently as he took a sip. "Whoa! That is bitter! *Bleh!*"

"Ha ha ha! I warned you. But you get used to it and the next thing you know, it's something special. If you give it a chance, it has some nice qualities."

Len caught the waitress' eye as she monitored the patio area. "I'll have a Campari with orange juice and a little ice, please," he said.

"You are a good sport," said Danielle. "You probably wouldn't want to know what they put in Campari to make it that red colour."

"Do I have to guess?"

"Yes. But I'll give you a good hint. Do you know what *Carmine* is?"

"An opera about a loud Spanish lady?"

"No, not *Carmen.* Carmine."

"Now you're just messing with me. You said the same thing twice."

No, car-*mine*."

"*Ohhhh*," said Len, feigning innocence. "You mean like Carmine Lake? I have a tube of Carmine Lake oil paint in my old paintbox, I think. They make Campari from old oil paint? No *wonder* it tastes like that."

"You're a terrible tease. But I think you don't know where carmine red oil paint gets its colour."

"It's a sort of magenta-red powder, isn't it?"

"It is. But where do you think that red powder comes from, *hmm?*"

"Uh, is it somewhere nice or somewhere horrible?"

"Well, that depends if you like bugs."

"What? Insects?"

"Yes, called the *cochineal*. Apparently, they made this bright red dye from those poor little bugs. But you're safe. I think they stopped using *cochineals* a few years ago. But maybe this is an old bottle!"

"I see what you're doing. You're telling me a big fib to see if I'm gullible, is that it?"

"It's true, I swear. They only stopped using the *cochineal* to make it red around 2006."

"So *maybe* I won't barf after all? This is sounding better and better."

She was really enjoying the game. "But wait. Hear that? That's the sound of them grinding the little bugs up. You're really lucky to get the real thing."

"So, do they drink this bug juice everywhere in Italy, or just in the part you went to?" he asked her.

"They told me they drink it everywhere. But maybe they were tricking me! They only give it to the tourists. And then they secretly laugh at us. Oh those sneaky Italians!"

"Well, I think we've got them figured out now. Which city was it?"

"I went on the train to Milan. It's about 7 hours from Paris by train. It is a lovely city but I spent too much money there. I was having a little bit too much fun shopping, I think. Milan is just a little to the east of the town of Novara, where Campari was created, you know."

"Well, I've always wanted to go to Italy, so I'd better get used to the Campari, eh?"

Danielle watched as the waitress stepped out onto the patio with a bright red drink on her tray. "I think that one's for you. I hope you like it." She lowered her voice to a conspiratorial whisper. "Oh, and don't look, but those people sitting down over there are probably Italians, getting ready to have a good laugh at the Londoners."

The waitress set down the tall red glass garnished with a slice of blood orange. Len lifted the drink. "Cheers!"

In the afternoon sun, Danielle's hair shone like gold as she raised her glass. "Here's to London Town," she said and flashed that radiant smile.

"I thought you lived in Paris?"

"Oh I do, but not this summer. I found a lovely little houseboat for rent and so I'm living here until the end of August. I wanted to work on my English and meet some new people, you know?"

"Well, I'm very glad you did," said Len. "Cheers!"

Danielle tool a sip and gazed at the liquid in the glass for a moment, as if distracted. "Thanks for meeting with me. I wanted to talk to you about something." She leaned closer and lowered her voice. "Remember when you were asking about that girl we met, Zena?"

"Yes. Why do you ask?"

"I didn't really tell you the whole story about that. I told you what she said when she and I went to the lavatory—I mean the ladies room—at that nice restaurant. She asked me if I am an escort, which surprised me a little. It upset me a bit, you know?"

"Of course. You say there's more to the story?"

"Well, I didn't tell you everything she said to me," she explained, "because she asked me to promise not to say anything. So, I thought maybe it was, I don't know, some kind of test or something from Alec. You know, I think he is a bit suspicious sometimes."

"I hope it's not a mistake to tell you," Danielle said. "She told me that *she* is an escort. Is that the same thing as a hooker? I don't really know these things too much. It's a private thing, I know. It's not really any of my business. You don't have to tell me."

"There's really nothing to tell," said Len. "I don't know too much about escorts myself, but it seemed like she was just being friendly and polite. It's a not a bad business, I suppose, being paid to be a good conversationalist at dinner parties."

"Oh, come on. You don't think an escort does more than that? The men must assume there are, you know, options available."

"I suppose, but she didn't offer and I didn't ask." Len didn't know too much about hookers either, but he was pretty sure they were a lot more forthcoming than Zena had been.

"Well then, you are a nice gentleman," Danielle said. "I can tell you for sure that when some men have paid for a woman's expensive meal and the nice wine and all that, they think they deserve some, you know, *payback*. Like they are entitled. Sometimes a girl just has to get out of the car, you know? It's not easy."

"I think it's quite common for unkind men to act badly around beautiful women."

She fluttered her eyelashes. "Oh, you think I'm beautiful?"

Len smiled. "Yes, yes, I do. There, I've said it."

"Well, that's nice of you to say that. But yes, I think you are right about men who are acting badly. Those guys who think they've got it made, but they don't have any...." She paused, searching for the right word: "*empathy*. They don't know what women like. Or they don't care. Well, maybe some women like guys who act like that. But that's messed up."

"You just like a *little* bit bad, right?" He said with a wink.

"I can always tell when a guy is not a nice person deep down in his soul. I just watch the way he treats strangers. Those guys who are jerks, they don't ask nicely. They demand things, they order people around."

"I've met a few women like that, too."

"Yes, of course. I didn't mean to say it was only men. Believe me, women are worse when it's just girls around. But it's the way the big shot guys act around me that I notice."

She ran her finger around the rim of her glass. Len was trying to think of something worthwhile to add when she continued. "I was a bit confused and maybe a bit jealous when *she* was in the car when he came to pick me up, you know?" Danielle admitted. "I thought maybe she was some other girlfriend or something. Alec just introduced her as a 'friend' of his. Or I thought maybe I had done something wrong that night when you and I first met at that big art show place, when he sent me home alone. I can usually understand why guys do the things they do, but he really surprised me, sending me home like that. Now I wonder if maybe he was meeting someone else later that night."

Len thought back to that night that he and Georgia had

lost track of the others. That was the night that Alec, Johnnie, and Dal had done the *robots* wall painting. Apparently, Danielle hadn't been told about *that*.

Again, Danielle cycled back onto the subject of her insecurities about Alec and Zena. "I think maybe she felt my confusion and that's why she explained to me that Alec did not want you to know—that's what she said. He *is* a friend of yours, isn't he?"

"I don't know," said Len. "I thought so." Maybe these sorts of mind-trips were how guys like Alec manage to snag nice-looking women, Len thought.

"Maybe I shouldn't tell you all this," she said, rather belatedly.

"No, I'm glad you did, really. Where did you say the boat was?"

"Oh, it's pretty close to here, in Islington, on Regent's Canal. In that area called The Angel, you know?"

"Yeah, nice. Lucky you."

"I know!" She beamed. "The boat is a bit petite, you know, but she's got a very cute name. The Ark Angel. She's pretty old, but I like her. She's just what I was looking for."

"Your own tiny ark, *vrai bon*."

"I was thinking of going back there now. Why don't you come with me and you can see her for yourself?"

"Yeah, I'd like that."

"It's nice to have some company. I don't really like taking that tube-train alone sometimes."

She finished her drink and slid the glass toward the middle of the table. "Ready to go?"

* * *

They walked together from the hotel to the Old Street station. From there, it was a 13-minute tube trip to the Angel Station at Islington High Street and then a pleasant walk through the terrace gardens to the canal.

When they got to Colebrooke Row, they walked past the ironwork gate down a sloping ramp to the canal. "Here it is," she announced. "The Ark Angel." It was an older style houseboat, tidier than most, painted in two shades of blue. On top of the cabin area were several potted plants.

"It's not much of a vegetable garden, but it looks nice, hey? Come on board. Be careful of that rope."

"I see you have solar panels. Very eco-friendly, good for you."

"Ah, they don't work very well. They power the lights and my *réfrigérateur*—what is it, a frigidaire?—and my little stereo but that's about all. I have to run the generator if I want a cup of tea. So I kind of gave up on tea and coffee. Make yourself comfortable."

She opened a sliding window. "You have a girlfriend?" she asked.

"Nah, not really."

"You were with Georgia for a while there, weren't you?"

"We just had a few laughs, you know? I don't think she wants a steady boyfriend. She was married, you know."

"Oh, you have gossip, too?" she teased.

"No, I don't kiss and tell."

"But you like girls, right?"

"Oh yeah, oh, definitely. Yeah."

"It's pretty cozy here, but it's a bit hot sometimes. I have to open these vents here. That's better."

"You want to have a drink with me? I have some nice white wine. I hope it's cold enough for you."

"White wine sounds good to me."

She poured two glasses and handed one to Len.

"Cheers" she said. "It's okay?"

"Perfect," he replied.

"You like to kiss me?"

"Hmmm…" Len put on a quizzical expression, feigning a tough decision.

"Alec didn't put you up to this to test me, I hope," he imagined himself getting slapped in the face for saying. Instead, he just smiled and hoped.

"You're very funny, I think. But it's okay. No one will bother us. Come with me."

* * *

At 4:48 the next morning, Len got dressed and pulled on his boots before Danielle was awake. The first light was breaking as he opened the cabin door and stepped out onto the houseboat deck.

He threw his arms over the top of the cabin and stretched. As he did this, he noticed the brick face of the canal tunnel cast a nearly perfect reflection in the water below.

Suddenly he was being roughly picked up by the jacket. The next thing he knew, Len hit the chilly water. As he paddled to the dockside, he coughed out the water he had inhaled in a panic. Above him stood Alec, glowering.

"Fuck you Len. You think I wouldn't find out about this? Stay away from her."

Danielle poked her head up from the galley. "What the fuck, Alec? I'm not your property and I'll sleep with whomever I damned well please." She looked at Len, hanging onto the mooring rope. "Help him out of the water for God's sake. Then go home and get some sleep. You need to rethink your priorities."

"He can get himself out of the water." He pointed a finger menacingly. "Don't cross me, Lennie."

As he strode off, Danielle shouted. "And don't come here again."

Len pulled himself out of the water and was sitting in a puddle on the dock when she stepped off the boat with a beach towel and sat next to him. He couldn't help but laugh. "Omigod, what a way to start a day."

* * *

Alec spent most of the next two days in his room at home. No word from Duckie. No chatter from the crew. No responses from Danielle. And now things with Len were probably screwed up, too. On the evening of the second day, there was a polite *knock knock* on the door.

"Go away, please."

His father's voice replied. "Can I have a brief word with you, son?"

Alec sighed and spoke to the door. "I don't really feel like talking much, dad."

"I know, son. I was just wondering if you could help me with a couple o' things down at the workshop. There's loads to do, and I'd sure appreciate your help with a couple. Like that great table we made, eh? I've got another one that needs fixin'... Do you think you could spare a few hours to help your old dad? I'll pay you, of course."

"Yeah, okay dad," Alec said listlessly. "I'll come down to-morrow morning."

* * *

The next morning, Alec's cellphone buzzed. He hurried over to the streetside window of the flat and pulled the curtain aside as he answered. Duckie's silver and blue limousine was double-parked outside. "Shit!" He answered the phone and spoke as nonchalantly as he could manage: "Alec here."

"Come outside immediately," said the voice. "The car's out front." Alec sniffed his shirt. He hurriedly pulled it over his head and put on a clean one, gargled a shot of mouthwash, combed his hair, grabbed his house keys and pulled the door shut.

Alec's front door opened and he stepped onto the porch, then turned to lock the door. In her BMW across the street, Georgia shook a sleepy Len awake. "Finally! There he is. He's coming out."

They both slid lower in their seats, peeking out from behind a map Georgia held in her hands. As Alec approached the Daimler, the rear door opened. He swung it open and climbed in.

"Hullo Duckie." Silence. "Top of the morning to you, Bill," said Alec, as cheerfully as he could manage. Neither one of them said anything.

After an extremely awkward pause, Duckie said, "Let's go for a ride, shall we?"

Bill put the car into gear and drove away. As the car began to move, Len and Georgia sprang into action.

"I have no idea whose car that is," said Len, "or who that woman is, but I'll bet you it will answer some of our questions."

"Follow the money," said Georgia. "Here we go. Keep your head down," she said as the BMW pulled out on the street, a half-block or so behind the Daimler.

Len and Georgia were unaware that a white van was following *them*.

At 9:30 a.m., Alec's cell phone buzzed. "Where are you?" said the text from his dad.

* * *

Dal was having difficulty deciding what to do. Georgia and Len were following Alec, but why? Were they part of a plan he'd not been invited to participate in? Alec had been awfully quiet lately. Dal wondered: Is he mad at *me*?

Mostly, Dal was unsure about whether he should let Alec know that he was being followed. Perhaps he should ask Georgia and Len what they were up to. Or perhaps he should just stay concealed and investigate. Revealing oneself seemed a very un-invisible thing to do.

Dal followed the BMW up through NW3 past Hampstead Heath. In their car, Georgia and Len were careful to keep their distance from the Daimler. Finally, its turn signal flashed. It pulled into a driveway on Redington Road. The BMW came to a stop and backed into a parking spot just outside the expansive property's black iron gate. At the far end of the block, Dal found a parking spot for the van and adjusted his mirror to watch the other cars.

"Whoa," said Georgia. "If *this* is Alec's parents' house, then they really *are* rich."

"That looks like a very expensive car, too," added Len. "I'll bet you that's his mum."

"Or maybe a wealthy lady friend?" Georgia hypothesised. "There's a guy driving, too—maybe that's his dad. I didn't really get a good look at him."

"Here's your chance."

They watched as the driver's side door opened and Bill stepped out of the car. He opened the Daimler's rear door and Alec and the Duchess got out. She tugged at her dress as Bill locked the car, then opened the front door of the house and stepped inside to hold it for them.

In the car outside the gate, Georgia peered through a pair of binoculars as Bill closed the front door. "I can't believe it," she said. "It's Bill. That *bitch*."

The Duchess walked briskly through the front foyer. "Come with me," she said firmly.

Alec followed her up the stairs and straight into her bedroom. "Take off your clothes," she commanded.

As he undressed, she slipped off her dress and from the second drawer of an ornate dresser near the bed pulled a handful of silk handkerchiefs.

"Lie down and put your hands up there." As he lay on the bed, she began tying the silks around his wrists. She then wrapped them around the bed posts and tied a knot.

"I've been thinking about you," she said as she straddled him and teased him with another of the silk kerchiefs. "Would you like to be blindfolded or gagged?"

Alec quickly ran through the possibility of answering questions (at the very least!) while being gagged and decided that being blindfolded was preferable.

"I'd like to commission a new piece from you. Have you got anything on the topic of absence?"

"Absence as in nonexistence or absence as in the state of being away from a place or person?"

"An absent lover, perhaps. Could be absence of respect, absence of responsibility, absence of care and attention, absence of law and order, government, or something big like that. I don't want anything silly, like a missing tooth or that sort of thing."

"I understand. I'll put some ideas together to show you."

Four pairs of empty handcuffs cuffed to a brass bedframe would be right on the nose, thought Alec.

Inside a front pocket of the pants lying by the side of the bed, Alec's cell phone buzzed as a new text message appeared. "You've been followed."

* * *

Len and Georgia took turns with the binoculars, but there wasn't much to see other than the car out front and a pile of wood and a tarp at the side of the house. A light was turned on behind one of the curtained windows on the second floor, but after 20 minutes or so, it turned off again. Georgia was getting impatient.

Len was studying the upper-floor windows through the binoculars and Georgia was looking at the house when suddenly there was a *thump thump thump* on the sidewalk-side window behind them. They both jumped in fright. A tall figure leaned down. It was Dal. Georgia rolled down the window. "Jesus Christ," she said. "You nearly gave me a heart attack."

"What are *you* doing here?" Dal asked them.

"Might ask you the same question," said Len, evasively.

"We are wondering what Alec is doing here, said Georgia matter-of-factly. "Do you think this is his parents' house?"

"I don't think so," said Dal. "I've met his mum and dad. They live back where that car first picked him up. It's where I usually pick him up, too."

"You really startled us," admitted Len. "You were following us the whole way?"

"Yeah," said Dal, distracted. "You know, I don't think Alec is gonna be very happy about this."

"Well," Len smiled wanly, "we don't have to tell him, do we?"

"We were wondering if maybe he was in some kind of

trouble," added Georgia, realizing that this didn't sound as much like a fib as she'd thought it might.

"Yeah…" mumbled Dal. He suddenly wished he could un-send that text he'd sent.

* * *

Thirty minutes later, Dal received a one-word reply from Alec.

Who?

Dal tried out several explanations in his head, but he couldn't decide if they were any good. The only one that seemed to be genuinely good was the one where Alec thanked him for setting a good example and telling the truth. But he worried that telling the truth would get Len and Georgia in a lot of trouble—maybe even kicked out of the crew. He didn't want to be responsible for breaking up the dream team.

He responded to the text. *It was me.*

Go home now, came the reply. *I will contact u.*

"I'm going to leave now," Dal told Len and Georgia. "I'm not feeling so good."

Georgia watched him walk away back down the block.

"I think we should leave, too," said Georgia. "I'm not sure there's anything else we can accomplish here, short of going up there and knocking on the door. And I'm sure as hell not going to do that."

"Do you think Dal will tell Alec?"

"I'm absolutely sure he will."

"Well then, we are rightly and royally screwed."

Nine

Finding Morals

Later that afternoon, Dal was in his garage at home with his protective goggles and gloves, a heat gun and a pair of tin-snips. He was snipping pieces of coloured plastic from bottles and other plastic containers and melting them onto a board with the heat gun, producing a colourful and slightly three-dimensional collage of repurposed plastic waste. And when you looked at the object from a distance, it became obvious that the placements weren't random. They were images of endangered species of animals.

His phone buzzed. It was Alec. He pulled off his gloves and slid the goggles up onto his forehead. "Hullo."

"What the hell were you thinking? And who were you with?"

"It was just me. I was alone in the van. I just wanted to know who that lady is I've seen you with sometimes."

Alec was outraged. "You've been spying on me?"

"No. You taught us how to be invisible. I was just prac-tising and that fancy limousine arrived and you came out of the house and jumped in. And I was curious, as I think you would be too. You know, if you don't want people to know who you're meeting with, you shouldn't have them park their fancy cars in front of your house."

It was hard to argue with Dal's logic. "Well, you're right," admitted Alec, in a rare display of humility. "That was my mistake. I will be more careful in the future. However, the people I meet with are my business alone and I will not tolerate being followed or having my private affairs discussed by others without my permission. Was I not clear when I said that what I do—what the team does—is a secret?"

"Yes... I mean no," said Dal, sulkily. "I understand."

"You know the rules, Dal, and I'm afraid there can be no preferential treatment because we're friends."

"I know," said Dal. "I'm sorry."

"I must ask you to promise not to mention anything about this woman or attempt to contact her in any way. This is very important, Dal. I want you to promise me that."

"I promise," said Dal.

"I know I owe you some money. Is 50 enough?"

"Nah, don't worry about it."

"Look, I know the guys in the crew are your mates, and I respect that. I can't stop you from being their friend. But you're officially out of the crew, effective immediately. I thank you for your service and I ask that you don't discuss crew business with the others."

"Is this permanent," asked Dal, "or do you think there's a chance I might be able to rejoin at some point?"

"I dunno, Dal. We'll keep in touch."

After he hung up, Alec reflected on what Dal had said about Duckie parking in front of his house. She had *never* done that before.

* * *

Dal has left the crew, said the text message from Alec. *We still consider Dal a friend, of course, so please continue to be a good friend to him, but please do not discuss crew issues or concerns with Dal until further notice.*

As soon as he saw the message, Len telephoned Georgia. "Hey," he said, "did you see that message from Alec? Dal's been kicked out of the crew!"

"What!? No!" she said. "I'm at work. Why Dal?"

"I dunno," said Len. "It's hard to tell, but it sounds like Dal took the blame and left us out of it entirely."

"Really?" The line went silent for several seconds. "That doesn't seem right."

"You know," she said after another long pause, "I promised myself I wouldn't do guilt trips anymore. And I'm having one right now. So fuck that. I'm owning this."

"Uh, what do you mean? Do you want me to confess, too?"

"No, no, God no. You do whatever your heart tells you to do. This is my guilt trip, not yours."

Georgia phoned Alec and owned up to her role in what happened. But she insisted Dal was completely innocent, and she swore (and truly believed) that Dal was only looking out for Alec's best interests in sending that message. She left Len out of the picture entirely.

And so Georgia was dismissed from the crew, just as

Dal had been. Alec sent around another message, advising the others—as he had with Dal before—that their friendship with her was encouraged, but they should no longer discuss crew business with her. Despite this, Georgia missed the brainstorming meetings, and she especially missed the extra money that her activities with the crew brought in. And, despite all the drama, she missed the weekly adventures that always seemed to be happening when they were around. Len might not have been boyfriend material, but he was fun to be around.

Her life at the gallery—now six days a week, since she'd had to lay off Bernice—seemed strangely like being in limbo. She found it increasingly difficult to muster fake enthusiasm for pictures or neon pieces she wasn't particularly fond of when customers expressed interest in them. This, predictably, only escalated her increasingly dire financial situation.

Georgia remembered when her relationship with Bill was going down the pan. Her mother, although living through a tragic situation of her own, had offered her some comfort by saying that she believed this was just life's way of making room for new growth. "If you can accept that everything happens for a reason," mom had said, "then change is just an opportunity for new growth."

Georgia's mom had certainly been through enough changes: a new house in a new city, a new school for Georgia, the new gallery, and then the biggest change of all, when Georgia's dad got sick and everything seemed to come undone. But mom was always good about not making everything about herself. Through it all, she was there for both

Georgia and her dad, a beacon in the storm, guiding Georgia through a tempestuous marriage to a much older man, a difficult divorce, Harry's death and a thousand other things that, when you're young, seem too huge to manage. Mom was living proof that Georgia was loved and lucky.

Mom said her philosophy was that all relationships tended to drift as people change and grow. It wasn't entropy, she said; it was more like moving downstream, keeping up with the changes.

Even so, it was hard for Georgia not to imagine that she was somehow to blame for her married friends' casual indifference, now that *their* lives had changed more than, it seemed to them, hers had. She'd invite them over for old times' sake, but they always seemed to be doing other things. Married people things. New parent things. New job things. She found herself wondering whether Dal was ever welcomed back.

She sat in her office at the gallery and dialed the phone.

On the other end of the line, her friend answered. "After Midnight here."

"Hey," she said meekly. "It's Georgia."

He heard it in her voice. "Hey, what's wrong?"

"I really need a friend right now, I guess." She wiped away a tear.

"I'm glad you called. Are you at the gallery?"

"Yeah, till five."

"Listen, I'll be in your area this afternoon. Can I come down there for a visit?"

"That would be great," she said. "I'll see you soon."

At five o'clock sharp, After Midnight, wearing sunglasses

and a Hawaiian shirt, pulled up in front of the gallery in his Cadillac.

"Are you ready to go?" he asked Georgia. *I have been since 3:30*, she thought.

"Absolutely," she said as she locked the door of the gallery and hopped into the passenger seat of the car. She thought back to the old days, when she first met him, just after he—and the car—arrived from Canada. "I remember you used to say it was hard to get used to the steering wheel being on the other side when you drove British cars. What about now? Does the steering wheel on the other side feel normal or strange now?"

He shrugged. "I dunno. I hardly ever drive British cars." He caressed the dashboard and smiled. "'Cause she's my baby."

Truth be told, he didn't really care whether a car was left-hand or right-hand drive. It was *this* car that mattered—that's why he spent so much to have it imported. GM never made a right-hand drive model of this car (and American versions sold for ridiculous prices in the UK these days!), so he'd decided to bring it along.

Georgia put on a pair of sunglasses as the Caddy cruised down the A10. As they always did, people stopped what they were doing and stared at the car as it passed.

"I love it. We look like tourists," she laughed. "We should take pictures of them as we go by."

"Should? We *must!*" he shouted into the wind. "I'm ready for my closeup!"

Georgia pulled out her smartphone and began snapping images of the people they passed on the street.

"Anywhere in particular you'd like to go?"

"Anywhere at all," she said with a smile as she took a picture of him.

"Let's drive down Brick Lane. Lots of tourists there." He steered the car into the left lane and turned east on Bethnal Green Road. As she took pictures of him and their surroundings, she realised that After Midnight and his convertible had always been able to cheer her up, to reconnect her with her best self. And unlike most men, he was never demanding. He was an artist and a gentleman. Their relationship was symbiotic. And *fun*.

"Hey, what kind of food do you like these days?" he asked.

"Well, what I *like* and what I *eat* aren't necessarily the same. I *like* a good home-cooked meal like mom used to make. But I seem to mostly eat noodles."

"Oh you poor thing. You sound meat deprived. Are you still eating meat?"

"I have been known to feast upon flesh from time to time. When feeling deprived."

"Well, it just so happens I have a couple of nice steaks and a pack of mushrooms in my very own fridge at home that want to be cooked up and eaten. And I might be able to root about and find a veggie or two in there somewhere, as well. So, I could do 'em up in a vaguely similar way to something your mum probably did much better. How does that sound?"

"Perfect. Yum."

"We're off then," he said, hitting the turn signal.

* * *

Len's phone rang. He thought it might be Danielle. It was Petra. "Can I meet with you?" she asked.

"Sure. What's it about?"

"I'd rather discuss it in person if you don't mind."

"O—kay," said Len. "Where?"

"How about, ah, the drinking fountain at Hoxton Square? The one in the centre."

"Yeah, I know the one. I can be there in 30 minutes."

Len took the Old Street tube station and headed down Old Street, then made a left turn into Rufus Street and Hoxton Square. There, waiting at the fountain, was Petra.

"Hello Petra," said Len from behind her.

"Boo yourself," she said with a smile. "You startled me."

"Sorry if I'm late."

"You're not," she said. "I just got here myself."

"What's up?" he asked.

"I have to tell you something really important," said Petra, "but you need to promise me you won't tell anyone else. You have to solemnly swear not to say a word, especially to Alec." She looked at Len sternly, her brow furrowed.

Not this again, he thought. *Nobody can keep a secret around here.* He nodded.

After a moment, she added: "And don't tell Paul either. He already thinks I've been cheating on him, and I don't want to give him any more reasons not to trust me."

"Maybe you just shouldn't tell me," said Len. "I mean, I'm completely trustworthy, and I absolutely wouldn't say a word, but what's the value in telling me, uh... whatever this is about?"

A possibility he hadn't previously considered suddenly occurred to Len: *Does Paul think she's been cheating with me?*

Len decided not to think about what he would do if that situation presented itself.

There was no question: he *did* find her sexually attractive. Get out, thoughts!

A second too late, he realised she was talking. About *something*.

"Well, I have to tell you because, frankly, it affects you, and I really think you deserve to know what's really going on, because, well, it's important...."

Len was curious and suddenly more than a little worried, too. His mind raced over what seemed like a thousand possibilities. Was she leaving the crew? Breaking up with Paul? Pregnant? A cop?

"I-I appreciate that," he stammered, "and I'm honoured that you consider me a good enough friend to tell me." It had been a long time since he had been in the Friend Zone like this. "All right, before you tell me, though, can you tell me how *you* found out about this?"

"Sure."

Petra was looking increasingly rattled. "Can we walk around the block? I really need to walk. Just once around the square."

"Sure, no problem. I've got all afternoon."

"Have you seen Paul's piece book recently?" she asked. (Odd question to start with, thought Len.)

"Can't say I have. I've seen Paul *with* it, though."

"Well, I took a look at it last week, and I realised that

several of Alec's recent designs were in Paul's book. But this is the strange thing: they looked like *earlier* versions. I think they might have been *Paul's* designs originally."

"And then I was talking to Johnnie and *he* mentioned that Alec had asked him to do some secret deal. So, I just thought...."

It occurred to Len that if he mentioned *his* secret deal with Alec to Petra, it was a virtual certainty that the news would spread at least as far as Johnnie. And heaven forbid that Dal should hear of it.

Petra pulled a leather-bound book emblazoned with a Celtic knot pattern out of her backpack and riffled through the pages until she found the one she was looking for.

She pointed to a page containing several pencil drawings. This one, she explained, was by Paul, just as the last design had been Johnnie's. She expressed regret that she had sold him one of her better designs, too. "But I needed the money at the time," she said. "I still sell him some of my simpler stuff now and then."

"Alec is making secret deals to acquire designs from all of you?"

"What was really interesting," Petra said, "was what happened next. I took another look at Paul's piece book just a couple of weeks ago, you know, after the night of that Moloko gig, and all of those pages were gone. They'd been *cut out* of the book. And I looked back through the older pages and there were a *lot* of pages cut out, which is weird because it's not the rough-looking stuff that's getting cut. So, I dunno," she said. "I just wanted to... sort of warn you, I guess, that maybe Alec isn't really the creator he makes himself to be, y'know?"

"Hmm. Thanks for the heads-up," said Len.

Alec, it seemed, had deals going with them all.

Len paged through her piece book. "Why don't you work up some of these ideas?" he asked. "They're great."

"I am actually working on this one right now," said Petra, pointing to a sketch of a figure sitting as if seeking shelter in a shadowy doorway. "I had this dream, you see, of this beautiful boy who has to go off to war. And it's like his dreams are all waiting for him but they are threatened. So he's like a star that's ready to shine, but surrounded by darkness. I'll have this dark doorway with this beautiful boy looking fragile but brave, in a cloak like a cosmic cloud—a star that's not yet fully formed. I don't know why, but the picture was called 'Stellengard' in my dream. So I think that's what I'm going to call it."

"I think 'stell' or 'stellen' means 'put'," said Len. "Is it a... oh, what do they call those compound words where two words are joined to coin a new word expressing a single concept?"

"A *portmanteau*?"

"That's it. So, something like a portmanteau of 'stell' and 'en garde'? That would be "to place on guard."

"Yeah, more or less."

"Sounds like a perfect name."

"I guess Paul's your beautiful boy?"

"I haven't quite decided. He is beautiful to me, of course, but I was imagining a face that really captured the innocence of youth. I dunno, maybe a slightly more androgynous look, with a hint of 'would have been a rock star' tragic quality."

"Hmm, that's pretty deep. I'll have some of whatever you were smoking," he said with a smile.

"No really, it was a dream. I could see the whole picture very clearly. The grey doorway, this thin figure with his head turned toward me, facing sideways with knees up, wearing this puffy looking cloak of stars like a brightly coloured cloud —and otherwise naked for reasons that honestly make no sense to me, but whatever—even its name. So, I'm just going to try to manifest that, you know?"

"Sounds great. I look forward to seeing it."

* * *

Everyone was surprised to everyone to learn that Alec had reached out to Dal and Georgia over the weekend and had invited them to rejoin the group. Johnnie was convinced that it had been at Len's insistence. This did sound plausible—but whatever the reason, they were all delighted to hear the news. There was a palpable excitement when Alec announced that he had a big job planned. It was, he assured them, a beautiful three-colour design, with a perfect wall to put it on. Len, he said, would be previewing the design at a planning meeting on Tuesday.

The day of the job, Dal arrived in the afternoon and drove the van into the bay at the back of the shop. Len rolled up the last of the stencils and helped Alec and Dal load the tarp, ladders and paint box into the back of the van. They checked their flashlights, ropes and the customised painter's tape dispensers Len had invented. Gloves, check. Fresh batteries in the walkie-talkies, check. At last the risks were mitigated, the plans set, the van loaded, the fake plates applied, and the other details attended to.

As it had been on the evening of the psyche fest at Moloko, the plan for tonight was to get hand-stamped and be seen at the Nufo club, slip away and complete the piece and then return to the club to cement an ideal alibi.

For reasons that weren't especially clear to the others, Alec made the decision to move the pre-planning meeting to Her Majesty's in Hoxton. This, he explained, would allow them to have a nice meal, work out any last-minute issues, and be close to both the club and the job site at Hoxton Square. This explanation didn't really make sense to Len, as the Stag's Head was also close to the square. But perhaps the food was better at this other place. And so the crew, minus Georgia, who had said she couldn't attend, met at Her Majesty's pub and grill at the usual time of 8 pm to go over the final details of the plan.

"With the extra ladders, we'll need all six of us unloading tonight," explained Alec. "It'll be two lookouts, two on the ladders, and two managing the stencils and paints. Len and Dal have got the van all packed up and ready, so when we get there—"

"Pardon me, Alec," said Johnnie. "May I say a word?"

"What is it, Johnnie?" Alec said, with a hint of annoyance in his voice.

This was unusual, thought the others. Johnnie *knows* that Alec doesn't like being interrupted during a planning session.

Johnnie gulped and then just blurted it all out, his voice quivering with overwrought emotion. "Petra," he said, his hand shaking, "I'm in love with Paul. I'm sorry I never told you this before, but it's the truth and I had to tell you."

"What—?!" said Petra, echoing what surely must have been the reaction in everyone else's minds around the table.

"Paul," said Johnnie, with tears welling in his eyes. "I need to be with you and if I can't be..." he gulped, "then, I can't be part of the group any longer."

Everyone was simply stunned by Johnnie's confession. Alec, in particular, looked shocked. Len had never seen an expression like that on his face.

"Oh dear, dear Johnnie," said Paul. "That's really sweet and I'm flattered—I really am. But I'm with Petra now." He looked at her. "And I think," he added, "she wants to be with me too."

Petra tried to think of something to say to Johnnie that didn't sound jealous or bitchy and realised that any talk of being "just friends" or saying anything about not wanting to share Paul's affections with anyone else would probably go over badly or at least muddy the waters. How had she never seen this before? And what did Paul mean by "...with Petra *now*"? Had he been two-timing *her* on the side with Johnnie?

Everyone just sat in silence for a moment. Johnnie sniffed and stood up. "I love you Paul," he said, sounding entirely miserable. "Goodbye." Before anyone could say anything else, he pushed his chair out, grabbed his jacket and walked away.

"Oh. My. God." Petra muttered, finally breaking the silence. She turned to Paul. "Do you want to go talk to him?"

"Jesus H. Christ," muttered Paul. "I knew he was… but…."

"Not just you, Paul," Petra reminded him, putting her hand on his.

"But we were just friends," he insisted.

Alec texted Georgia. *We are one person short tonight. Can u help us out?*

A few seconds later, she sent her response. *Sorry, I'm busy all evening. I wish everyone the best of luck.*

Alec put down his phone. "Well," he said, rubbing his hand through his hair as if trying to reorganise the thoughts in his head, "I guess we'll only have one lookout tonight."

Ten

All Change

To make up for Johnnie's absence, the mission planning meeting went on longer than usual—and it required changes to the duties of each of the participants. With fewer hands on deck in case something should go wrong, Petra would have to take over the ground floor ladder and rope duties as well as being a lookout, and Dal would have to help with more of the heavy lifting. The main point of discussion was how to make do with only one lookout—Dal suggested leaving the van parked below so that he could assist with the lookout duties, but the others deemed this unnecessarily risky. They decided it was much better to move the van as per the original plan, and have Len, Paul and Alec up on the roof to get the job done as quickly and efficiently as possible.

As he had become more involved in the minutia of the planning and preparation phases, Len became increasingly aware of the extraordinary efforts Alec went to in order to obfuscate certain parts of the operation. He always paid cash for the paints and any other equipment that was needed. He always paid *them* in cash. As a matter of fact, Len realised he had never even seen Alec use a cheque or a credit card. It was an odd way to do business, but the bills got paid.

After dinner that night, they all piled in the van and headed for the club. Dal dropped them off near the door, parked the van and was back before they reached the front of the line. Alec paid the admission fees, and they all got their hand stamps. After a half-hour or so of parading around, deliberately bumping into everyone they recognised, and dropping their names at the door, the bar and the coat-check room, they were ready to go. They slipped out the back and headed down the alley. A minute later, the van pulled around the corner and headed west toward Hoxton Square. Dal and Petra had the windows rolled down and surveyed the nearby windows and building as they approached the drop-off point. They declared it safe to proceed and Dal pulled the van into the loading zone beside the building. As Dal kept an eye on the side view mirrors, the others slid open the side door of the van and jumped out.

Paul and Petra ran around the back and opened the rear door. They helped Alec and Len lift the frame and the ropes for the cloak of invisibility out of the vehicle and onto the sidewalk. Up went Len, Alec, and Paul, taking with them the ropes and pulley they needed to raise the other gear. Once the ropes were attached to the pipes on the third storey, they pulled up the frame and the cloak up onto the roof. Then up went the stencils and the paint box. Petra and Dal stayed below and clipped the trestle ladders onto the pulley ropes, then pulled the ladders within reach of the three men onto the roof, where they were unclipped and moved into position. This was one of the trickiest parts of the operation, as the operation had to be done as silently and quickly as possible to avoid arousing suspicion. Fortunately, the maneuver was well practiced and everything went flawlessly.

Then Dal, doing double duty as driver and secondary lookout, jumped back in the van and moved it to the waiting area and exited the vehicle. On his way back to the building on foot, he hid the hats and hoodies disguise kits at the drop-off points and rechecked the nearby buildings and windows for signs of unexpected late-night activity that might interrupt their plans. Fortunately, the entire area was quiet and dark. 'Area checked out OK' he texted. 'In position' Petra confirmed. She checked the walkie-talkies. "Okay," said Dal. "Loud and clear," said Alec. (Too loud, in fact. He turned it down a little.)

The others, meanwhile, were still hoisting materials up onto the roof from behind the cloak. For these kinds of jobs, the fastest method of setting up a scaffold was to use two trestle ladders and a board. It was crude, but it was quiet and quick—and reasonably safe. They'd experimented with alternatives—Len's idea to use bamboo scaffolds with zip ties and cross braces was the most promising—but assembling and safety checking such a scaffold in the dark had so far proved insurmountably difficult. They usually needed ladders elsewhere anyway.

The team's ladders of choice were mostly of the telescopic variety. These were compact enough to hide in the van (much better than driving around trying to look inconspicuous with a couple of huge ladders on a roof rack!), and fairly light-weight. Best of all, they were super-quick to put up and pull down.

In the old days, they had used a plank suspended between a pair of ladders as a scaffolding platform. It was terrible in several ways, not the least of which was the fact that a plank of sufficient thickness to support two people was dauntingly heavy. But while developing his custom scaffolding proto-type, Len had come up with an aluminum design with hooks on each end that bounced less and was far lighter. It was the one part of the prototype that was foolproof enough to implement immediately.

Once the two trestle ladders were set up with the scaffold between them, the cloak of invisibility was pulled into place and they were able to get to work in earnest. The guidelines went up first, and then, once the precise positions of the first set of stencils was known, the first of the stencils were taped up (impressively quickly, thanks to that new painter's tape dispenser!) and the painting progressed at a rapid pace.

As the chief designer of the work, Paul was a key partici-pant and he did most of the finessing of the shading. He used the spray cans skillfully, as one would an airbrush. Up went the second set of stencils, organised by colour, and the appropriate paints were readied and applied. This was a three-colour job and they were already more than half finished.

Suddenly, the walkie-talkie crackled to life. "Police!"

Len, who was near the edge of the roof, dropped the two spray cans he was holding and looked down over the edge of the building at Petra. She pointed northward. Two police officers were on the roof of the adjoining building and were shining lights directly onto the area where the cloak was set up.

Alec, who had been readying a stencil mask near the top of the picture, was nowhere to be seen.

Paul, who was standing on the scaffold near one of the ladders, used it to clamber down onto the roof on the opposite side of the building from Petra. He looked around but couldn't see Alec. Nor was there any good escape route of this side.

"Shit!" hissed Petra into the handset from below. "I think you're about to get busted. Abandon ship. Get out of there."

When he heard this, Len grabbed the rope they'd used to haul the equipment up and checked that it was still securely tied around the drainpipe. He then threw the rope over the side of the building and slid down. Fortunately, his spray-painting gloves left him with only a mild rope burn.

Dal appeared from around the corner as Petra waited for someone else to appear at the top of the rope. Where the hell were they?

Paul finally appeared from behind the side flap of the cloak. He looked down at them anxiously, a spray can in his hand.

"Where's Alec?"

"You there," said one of the officers through a megaphone. "Put your hands up. Drop your weapon."

Paul dropped the can. "Slide down quick and meet us at the pickup point," Petra said into the walkie-talkie, as she and Dal ran away, not even stopping to grab a disguise.

Alec had climbed up onto the top rung of the ladder and

had managed to pull himself over the parapet at the top of the building. He kept low and crawled toward the emergency ladder at the exit point.

By this time, the police were practically on top of Paul. Alec, realizing that they were now between him and his escape route, decided to stay put and stay hidden. He pulled out his phone and began recording a video of what was happening below him.

As the cops closed in, Paul grabbed the rope and put one foot over the side of the building. Len watched in horror from below as there was a violent tug on the rope at the very instant Paul swung his weight over the side of building. He was shaken from the rope and fell very suddenly from the third storey, landing heavily with a sickening crunch on the pavement below.

The entire event was caught on video by Alec. When Paul didn't move at all for several seconds, Len ran over and put a hand on his chest. Alec watched in horror as Len, aghast, looked up in his direction. Around the corner from the front of the building, the two police officers were approaching from the north, their pistols drawn. One shouted at Len: "You there—get down on the ground or I'll shoot!" Len ignored the threat and ran to the corner of the wall just below Alec. The police were now standing over the fallen body with their guns drawn.

Alec waved his left arm over the side of the building. "Here, mate—catch." He dropped the phone down to Len. "Now run!"

Len ran away from the cops, heading south and then

ran a block westward, doubling back toward the Square. He jumped the park fence like an adrenaline-fueled hurdle jumper and hid in the bushes, then made his way north toward the pickup location. On the streets behind him, cops were swarming into the area. He headed northeast through the park and texted Petra and Dal: *Abort pickup plan. Leave the area ASAP.*

No one knew how he did it, but Dal got away in the van. Petra made a run for the nearest stash of disguise gear and managed to evade the police by keeping to the backstreets. Alec was not so lucky. He tried to remain hidden behind the parapet on the roof, but the police found him and dragged him off in handcuffs.

When Len got home, he looked around for a safe place to hide the phone. He finally decided that the top shelf of the pantry was probably safer than anywhere else. He then had to break the awful news of what he'd seen to the others.

Len felt that he should tell the others in person. Certainly, texting this news would be horribly crass. He decided to phone Petra first. Then Johnnie. Poor Johnnie would probably take this the worst of all, he thought.

"Hey Petra, it's Len," he said. His voice sounded like someone else's. "Where are you?"

"I'm walking north on the A10," she said, "fairly close to Georgia's house. What's going on? Did you get away all right?"

"Well, sort of. Listen, it's extremely urgent that I talk to you and the others."

Petra heard the panic in his voice. "What's wrong?"

"Well, I'd rather tell you in person. But can you do one super-important thing for me? *Don't* call Paul."

"Why the hell not?" she argued.

"I'm sorry, but I insist. Can you call Johnnie and Dal, and I guess Georgia too, and ask them to come over to the design shop? It's super urgent."

Now Petra was panicking, too. "What the hell's going on, Len? Can't this wait until the morning?"

"No, it absolutely *cannot* wait until the morning. Trust me, no. Just come to the shop, and I'll explain everything. I'll be there in about 10 minutes."

"All right," she said. "I'm on my way."

"I promise," Len said, "I'll tell you everything when I get there."

Ugh. Maybe texting would not have been as horribly uncomfortable as *that* was.

He texted the others. *SUPER URGENT. Come to the Lenz Design shop NOW. Respond when you see this message and come ASAP.*

Len made coffee and waited. Petra was the only one who showed up. He tried calling Johnnie and Dal, then Georgia. No answer.

Finally Dal texted back. "Sorry, I was driving around in the van," he wrote. "I'm on my way."

When Dal arrived at the shop, he apologized for not having the equipment. "Sorry about not picking up you guys," he said. "When I saw that message that said 'Leave the area,' I did exactly that."

"You did the right thing. Both of you," said Len. "Please,

sit down. I'm sorry to say I have some terrible news." A tear came to his eye. "Paul is dead."

Petra put a hand over her mouth in disbelief, a look of horror on her face. "Omigod, you can't be serious," she said, her hand shaking.

"I'm afraid I am. I saw him fall, and I checked for a pulse after he...." He couldn't finish the sentence.

Petra suddenly seemed to pull herself together. "What about Paul's parents? Do they know?"

"I dunno," said Len. "To be honest, I didn't know what to do, so I just ran. I left the scene. And I'm a witness." His lip trembled. "The cops saw me. They're definitely going to want to talk to me."

Petra looked up at the ceiling, her brow furrowed. "Poor Johnnie," she said quietly.

"That's what's I said, too," admitted Len, miserably.

Dal leaned forward and swallowed, then exhaled uneasily. "Sorry, I think I'm going to be sick," he said, getting up unsteadily. "Sorry," he said as he stumbled off to the washroom.

"I feel the same way, my friend," said Len. Now he had to tell them about Alec. He suddenly realized how little he really knew about Alec. No address. Not even a last name. "I guess we could find out what happened to Alec by contacting the police station," he said. "What's his last name?"

Petra shrugged.

There was the sound of running water for a moment and then Dal reemerged, wiping his face.

"Dal," said Petra, "What's Alec's last name?"

"He's never told me."

"This is ridiculous," said Petra. "Georgia *must* know. She went *out* with him."

"We have to think clearly about this," Dal said. "What exactly happened to Alec?"

"I wish I knew," said Len. I think the cops might have caught him. He was up on the roof. He threw me his phone. I've got it; it's safe."

"Did they see *you*?"

"I don't know," said Len. "Probably not. I didn't really see them. I only heard them and saw their lights."

Dal looked thoughtful. "So, you have Alec's phone? That could be good. There's a good chance that Petra and I—and maybe even you—won't be wanted for questioning, then."

"Yeah," said Len, "but I think Paul had a phone...."

"He did," confirmed Petra. "I don't think he had any of our addresses in it, though. Paul wasn't really big on addresses...."

Dal looked at Len and asked, "Do you think there's a chance Paul could be alive? Maybe just unconscious?"

"I wish. I really don't think so. He landed really hard—it was a horrible sound. I was too far away to catch him. I checked for a pulse, but...." Len's thoughts kept cycling back to that awful sound.

Dal moaned and held his head. "Do you think we should turn ourselves in?"

"I just don't know," said Len.

* * *

At the local police station, the police interrogated Alec for hours. They tried the usual good cop/bad cop tactics, and when those didn't work, they threatened to throw the book at him unless he gave them something. He pretended to be an underling and claimed that the ringleader got away, but when he claimed the big boss's moniker was "TCO," the chief said, "Well, we haven't got him. But we've got you, so we're going to pin it on you instead."

An abusive guard threw Alec into a jail cell with a couple of drunks.

The next morning, a SWAT team called the SCO19 Specialist Firearms Command broke down Alec's door and hauled away several external hard drives and computers, including his mum's MacBook.

They also confiscated his piece book. He was threatened with charges of malicious mischief, malicious destruction of property, conspiracy to commit criminal damage, criminal negligence causing death, creating a public nuisance, disturbing the peace, trespassing, breaking and entering, evading arrest, assaulting a police officer, and littering (!). And just to make sure the charges stuck, they planted a bag of narcotics in his room for good measure.

The story was front page news on every major newspaper from London to Manchester.

"Fatal fall kills local street artist"

"Vandals sought by police after fatal graffiti mishap"

"Police deny wrongdoing in graffiti caper"

As Alec sat on his uncomfortable gray cot in the jail cell, it suddenly occurred to him that this is what Duckie had meant when she said there was never a second chance. Duckie had set him up and now it was over.

She would see that the game went on without him. Her game didn't require any specific players—any team would do. It wasn't the collective organisation, it was *TCO* the persona that world cared about. The mysterious artist could never be tracked down because the persona was nothing but a front for a clandestine organisation. That was the real art. She'd select a new leader, ensure that he or she never learns too much, and keep winding up the clockwork.

The prison's visitor administrator called out the next name. "Mack...."

"Alec Mack, your father's here," announced the gaoler. The guard led him to the window.

"I'm sorry son," his father said. "We haven't got the money to pay your bond. They've set it so high, we're trying to get the amount changed to something more reasonable. But rest assured, we are working on it. We haven't forgotten you, son." The following Monday, a pretrial hearing for Alec's case was heard before a judge in court. Amongst the evidence presented by Alec's defense lawyer during the hearing as supposed proof that Alec's family didn't have pots of money was a set of receipts showing that Alec didn't pay for the tickets to get his crew members and Danielle into the Moloko the night of the *hallucidelia* art event—his father had given him five VIP tickets. The lawyer argued out that their attendance at this event proved that they were not the ones responsible for the property vandalism the prosecuting attorney had alleged was their doing that night.

* * *

Pundits speculated that, should the defendant be found guilty on all counts, he would likely be facing five to ten years in prison. Bookies took odds on fines versus incarceration. Sentiments on social media were all over the map. A group of wackos calling themselves free speech advocates argued that jailing artists was just the first step. Writers and video-makers would be next.

24 percent of those polled by one of the major dailies said they thought anything more than a 72-hour jail sentence for a wall painting was a bit excessive. 35 percent thought a jail sentence of 6-12 months was appropriate, with nine percent voting in favour of a sentence of two years or more—half of which, as some pointed out, could be spent outside a jail cell doing community work. 18 percent advocated making him clean up graffiti around the city, with eight percent expressing no opinion and 6 percent advocating the dropping of all charges.

Of the nine percent that advocated a lengthy jail term were some who wanted the judge to throw the book at him, to teach other would-be vandals a much-needed lesson on the sanctity of private property. And of course, there were death threats.

That night, Len was watching the evening news when an editorial piece came on that caught his attention. They were talking about the strange death of a local street artist and the investigation of the artist being held responsible. And there was Bob Mack, holding up a piece of paper he called evidence that Alec was gainfully employed with a 'legitimate' job. The camera zoomed in on the image and Len suddenly recognized it: It was the "Frankenstein's monster" copy of Len's original poster. For better or worse, no one seemed to make the connection between this piece and Len's original version. Len was alarmed to be so nearly exposed but relieved that no one was asking him for his opinion on the artistic merit of the copy.

His mother asked him if he'd heard a strange sort of electrical sound coming from the ceiling in the pantry area. "I'm concerned that it might be an electrical issue with the heater fan or something," she said. "You can't be too careful with that sort of thing, you know."

He retrieved Alec's phone from the top shelf and snuck it into his room for further examination. Its battery charge had finally given out. Fortunately, he had a compatible charger. An hour later, he turned on the now-partially recharged phone. Disappointingly, he couldn't figure out how to unlock it.

As if a wish had suddenly been granted, Len's phone rang. "Hello, is this Len?" said a familiar voice he couldn't quite place.

"It is. Who's this?"

"Lennie, it's Bob Mack, you've done some work for me, yeah?"

"That's me. Hello. I had no idea you're Alec's father."

"Yes. In fact, that's why I'm calling you. He says he gave you a phone. Do you still have it?"

"I sure do."

"Good. Alec says you'll want to take a look at a video on

that phone. He says the pin number you'll need to get into it is two-zero-zero-zero."

Of course it is, thought Len. "That's just what I needed. Thanks, Mr. Mack. By the way, is Alec still being held, or is he out on bail?"

I'm afraid they've set the bail fee so high we can't afford it. They've set it for fifty *thousand* quid. We've not got that kind of money, I'm afraid. We've got a lawyer working on getting the fee reduced. Alec thinks a video on that phone you've got there might help."

"I'll take a look right away and let you know if I find anything useful."

"Goodnight Len," he said. "Wish him luck."

2-0-0-0. Len unlocked the phone and reviewed the videos. It didn't take long for him to find the file from that fateful night on the rooftop. It was a grainy, birds-eye view of the rooftop area. Two policemen could be seen approaching from the adjoining roof, waving their lights and shouting. One shouted "drop your weapon" and suddenly they both had guns in their hands, pointing them at Paul. His hands raised, he dropped the spray can in his hand and lunged for the rope at the side of the building. As the police rushed over, he grabbed the rope and began to climb down the side of the building. The two officers grabbed the rope and violently pulled on it, in an apparent attempt to pull him back onto the roof. And then there it was: the fall. An unidentifiable figure crouched momentarily over the motionless body on the street below, then ran away into the darkness as more officers approached.

In a chilling final shot, two backlit figures approached with guns aimed at the lifeless body. Then the video ended.

* * *

Eleven

Who's Who?

As soon as the video had ended, Len sent a message to the others. *EMERGENCY MEETING! please convene at 9 a.m. at the fountain in Hoxton Square. Urgent!*

It was an unusual place to hold a meeting, but Len just couldn't imagine discussing this terrible tragedy with them in the jovial atmosphere of a bar. At least outside, they could let their feelings show. He didn't even know whether anyone would show up or whether they would even want to *see* the video. But he brought it anyway. Indeed, his own feelings were a muddled mix of anxiety, horror, and anger. The horrific images flashed through his mind on endless autorepeat: the sound of Petra's alarmed voice on the walkie-talkie, that moment of panic when they all scrambled, the policemen jerking the rope. He kept cycling through freeze-frames of the events—the guns, the rope, the fall. It felt like a setup.

The TV coverage was particularly worrisome to Len. He had been feeling increasingly paranoid ever since the TV broadcast showed that copy of his poster—sure, it was admittedly a very bad copy, but still, it seemed a glaringly obvious clue!—and now that literally millions of viewers had seen his anonymous hooded visage look up toward the camera in the now-viral video, people all across the country were speculating on who this associate of Alec's might be. As the name on the sign at *Lenz Design*—Alec's place of business!—he'd expected the cops to barge in there any minute for several days now and was frankly amazed that it hadn't happened yet. But it hadn't.

He arrived the square about 10 minutes early and paced back and forth along the walkway through the centre of the park. Dal and Johnnie arrived together and by 9 a.m., they were all there except Georgia. Len had sent her an invitation and had talked to her earlier in the week, but didn't expect to see her. After all, she had been dismissed from the crew by Alec. And she'd made it pretty clear that she no longer considered herself part of the group.

Len had gone over the agenda items in his head many times, but now, standing here in the square in the cold morning air, everything seemed different.

"It feels a little strange for us to be gathering without Alec here," said Len, "but I'm sure you'll all agree that this is a very serious situation. And I know the past few days have been terrible for you, but welcome back, Johnnie."

Johnnie had reacted with sheer disbelief when he'd heard the awful news about Paul. In the days that followed, he went from shock and disbelief to feeling guilty, angry, and depressed, then on down into a dark pit of despondency. Now he just felt numb, and that was an improvement.

"We need to get the truth out there," said Len. "We have proof that the police are lying."

"In case you were wondering, I feel there is a strong possibility that the Old Stag's Head is no longer a safe place for us to meet, given what came out in the news about the ownership of the pub."

"What was that?" asked Petra. "I don't have a telly."

"It was in all the papers," said Johnnie. "Alec's dad is one of the owners of that bar. So the cops are probably watching it, if they are looking for someone particular."

"Are they looking for us? Like, are we on a wanted poster somewhere?"

"I don't think so. We know that Paul and Alec were confronted by the police. Were any of you seen or confronted directly?"

The others shook their heads.

"That's good. As you know, Alec managed to capture a video of exactly what happened and he handed it off to me. I can't recommend it—it's horrible to watch. But it *is* important evidence and rather damning proof of actions taken by the police that were directly responsible for Paul's death. And it does provide proof of the involvement of certain parties— that is to say *me*—in the events that occurred that evening. So we've got to be really careful not to lose it or have it confiscated. I've made a backup of the video to iCloud. Do any of you have another type of cloud account that we can post it to?"

"There are lots of options, said Johnnie. I've got the

built-in one working on my PC, and I think GDrive or whatever it's called would probably work too."

Len tapped out a message on his phone. "I've just sent you all the URL". "But in case we get any questions from the media or lawyers, we need to decide who we say took these pictures. And I think it's a good idea not to mention any names or events in our communications that could incriminate others. At this point, it's probably not in Alec's best legal interests to cite him as the videographer."

"What about *anonymous*?" suggested Dal.

"We could make up a fake name," offered Johnnie.

"Hm, yes. Let's attribute it to TCO. That's the name Alec said belonged to the Big Boss."

"But shouldn't we be working with a lawyer or something to see that justice is done?" said Johnnie.

"*Fock* the justice system," argued Dal. "They're the ones that *did* this. I've had it with bleedin' police and so-called justice both. Paul was my mate and I'm fockin' mad now."

"Hear, hear," said Petra. It was right then and there that she decided that the video needed to be seen. As the others debated what to do, she uploaded the video to every video sharing website she could think of.

"But what about our cell phones, and all the surveillance cameras we must have passed on our way here? If the police really are looking for us, those fucking things will give us away for sure."

"That *is* a risk," admitted Len, "but I didn't really know what else to do. I figure that if the cops don't know who they're looking for and they haven't got any of our names or phone numbers, the risk is fairly low. Not zero risk, but it's not like we're international criminals. I don't think the cops have the resources to be one hundred percent focused on finding us. I hope."

"There's a much bigger risk of some other street artists getting arrested and making a bargain with the police to rat us out. *That* wouldn't surprise me a bit. So I advise you to think about any other taggers or graff artists you might've worked with or talked to about *Dreamteam*. If they have your address or phone number, you should be careful."

"I'm mostly worried," he added, "because of the way Alec got caught. It seems a bit suspicious, like the coppers knew we'd be there or something. So, I think there's a chance that someone deliberately ratted us out on that job. And until I've had a chance to talk to Alec about who that might be and what they might know, my advice is to try to protect your assets and minimise your risks if the feds *do* come calling."

"You know the drill. Avoid Old Bill," said Dal.

Petra thought for a moment and said, "I think I know who might have ratted him out."

"You don't think Georgia…?" said Johnnie.

"Oh God, no," said Petra. "No way. I think that woman we heard on the boat might have been angry enough to rat him out, though."

"Danielle?" Unlikely, thought Len. *Follow the money.*

"I think it might be that older woman Georgia and I saw Alec with. That day you followed us, Dal. Georgia called her a bitch, although she never really explained why. God, I wish she were here. I'll have to ask her about that."

"Yeah, about that woman" said Dal. "Alec told me never to mention her or attempt to contact her. Oops, I guess I just mentioned her."

"This woman is probably not a friend," said Len. "I'll try to find out more—and I'll keep your name completely out of it, Dal."

"No worries."

By the end of the meeting, the crew had split into two factions: Petra and Len argued in favour of anarchic action; on the other side, Dal and Johnnie expressed concerns about possible legal ramifications.

The video was incredibly damning, showing the police pointing their guns at Paul at the edge of the building and then seemingly shaking him off the rope as he attempted to climb down.

And then there was that final, horrible image of his broken and lifeless body lying in the street, made all the more poignant as the camera zoomed out to show the cops standing there, pointing their pistols at the body.

Len sent them all a link to the uploaded copy of the video and they shared hugs and a few tears before saying goodbye. That evening, Petra sent back a link to an edited version of the video, into which she'd inserted a short text message at the end. "Police testified under oath they weren't touching the rope" it said, as the clip playing in slow-motion proved otherwise.

* * *

One day later, the video had been banned from several sites for "graphic violence" but had still managed to rack up more than 14 million views and the media was all over the story and its seemingly incontrovertible evidence of police brutality.

Suddenly, the video was everywhere. They were covering the story in North America. The rising tide of dissent was suddenly a tsunami. The video catalysed public sentiments into mass demonstrations, calling for an end to police ultra-violence.

In reaction to the widespread defacement of trains, buses, buildings and other public surfaces occurring during the demonstrations, lawmakers responded by upping the maximum penalties for graffiti writing: 12- to 17-year-olds were subject to as much as 24 months of detention, while adults could be facing a sentence of up to ten *years*. For writing graffiti.

Then, armed with surveillance camera evidence, the police began hunting down the perpetrators of what they were now calling a conspiracy.

Inspired by Petra's actions, Len led an effort to produce a "truth tabloid," explaining what really happened. He enlisted his friends in the printing business to help and he and Petra created the editorial content.

* * *

COPS KILL STREET ARTIST screamed the front-page headline. Just beneath it, **Met Police Face Street Art Showdown** was an editorial piece calling for public action. On the flip side of the folded paper, **KILLED FOR ART** was a headline large enough to be read nearly a block away. A banner on the top of the four-page newssheet advertised the stories as "eyewitness accounts." And when the four-pager was unfolded, a giant poster-sized reproduction of the "MISS-ING" stencil piece filled the backside of the paper.

The eyewitness accounts blamed the cops for the murder of Paul Knightley; closeup photos pulled from the video provided incontrovertible proof that the police had lied under oath. In the most disturbing shot, Knightley, with nothing but a spray can in his hand, has his hands up as two heavily armed police point their pistols at him at point-blank range.

Another damning photo showed cops standing over the fallen body, their pistols drawn.

This image was iconified in a series of stencils and stickers bearing the caption RECORD EVERYTHING. The dreamteam made these items freely available on their website as part of their awareness campaign.

The dreamteam crew and Danielle all helped Len distribute the printed papers, and Johnnie created a website dedicated to the cause. On social media, they offered free bundles of papers to anyone else who wanted to help distribute them. Thousands did. They raised enough money to print and fold 750 bundles of the four-page newssheets.

Soon, the giant poster and the stickers began appearing all around the city, pasted onto construction site fences, billboards, walls and anywhere else they would fit.

It wasn't the image or the defiant graffiti that frequently accompanied it that drew the most attention, though. The deliberately sensational headlines caught the attention of local and national news media and the newspapers and radio talk shows frequently quoted from the tabloid while discussing the latest news about the case.

The lawyer attempted to keep Alec out jail by arguing that house arrest was just the thing to track a person predisposed to painting buildings and private properties in the middle of the night. But the argument didn't convince the judge, who ruled that house arrest provisions of the law are designed to restrict the movements of those where the authorities say they can't be kept in jail. And despite his lawyer's best efforts, the judge said this did not apply in Alec's case. Unbelievably, the conspiracy charge was upheld and he was sentenced to 3 years imprisonment.

The only bright spot in all this was the fact that Alec was found not guilty of the criminal negligence charge when the judge found the police more directly responsible for the death. That caused a firestorm in the media. Paul's parents filed a suit against the police.

The police maintained they weren't touching the rope at the time but the video clip Len supplied proved this claim false.

An inquiry was ordered. The media lionised the topic. The vandalisation of the city was seen as both symptomatic of social decay and a contributor to it. Suddenly, displays of force of any kind by the police came under fire. Activists reshaped the narrative to fit whatever variety of social justice they were seeking. A disproportionate number of victims were poor or black or gay, or homeless, or immigrants, or... you name it. The manufactured outrage bubbled over into demands by some for a murder verdict for the police officers responsible.

Interviewed in his cell by a reporter for BBC One, Alec said, "Obviously, I was most upset about seeing my good friend fall to his death after being shaken off a rope by the police. And having them attempt to suppress the facts of this case by lying under oath is of course, despicable behavior that I condemn in the strongest possible manner. I am, however, particularly disappointed by their subsequent actions, which include blatant attempts to shift the blame and responsibility for their actions onto the victims of their harassment. I call for all those responsible to be held accountable for these heinous actions in a court of law. And I call upon the public to stand against oppression and demand an end to police ultra-violence!"

"And what about the felony conviction? Will you be appealing that?" asked the interviewer.

"I've been advised by legal counsel not to talk about plans for an appeal. I will say, however, that I fully intend to pursue justice for the wrongful death of my friend and associate, artist Paul Knightley, and I ask that the British public do the same. These heavy-handed actions by jackbooted thugs in police uniforms are just the most visible examples of an out-of-control police state willing to lie to the public to conceal its own criminal agenda."

As soon as he heard this, the director had cut the audio feed and ordered the interviewer to end the interview. Alec continued to speak, until he noticed the camera's red tally light turn off.

To her credit, the interviewer waited until Alec finished speaking to thank him.

The next day, the newspapers revealed that Alec's father

was a part owner of the Old Stag's Head pub and had declined to put up bail for his son.

Social media activists called for a boycott of that business. Business at the pub increased. A photo of the *dreamteam* table in the pub made the newspapers. Art critics began discussing works attributed to the team—a list which included several pieces they hadn't had a hand in.

The video clip continued to attract millions of viewers and stirred a public revolt.

Protesters against police brutality convened at Hoxton Square with banners and signs decrying the violence. "Who killed Paul" the crowd chanted as they marched through the streets and around Shoreditch, in what the BBC characterised as "an ironic twist to the old 'Paul is dead' Beatles conspiracy theory."

The iconic image of Paul, with his spray can raised high over his head, appeared everywhere. It was on T-shirt and hoodies, flags and "PAUL IS DEAD" posters.

An image of a protester wearing a black face mask and an "ART CAN'T BE SILENCED" T-shirt made the front page of *The Times*.

The Metropolitan Police Service released a statement saying the officers involved in the incident had been suspended without pay 'pending further investigation,' but it did little to ease the tensions on the streets. As police forces hunted down graffiti writers and clashed with protesters, other instances of alleged police violence raised tensions even higher. Angry protesters began smashing windows and defacing walls and signage throughout the city. Videos of people using a spray can and a lighter to create a makeshift flamethrower led to warnings not to try this, but of course the kids did it anyway.

As tensions escalated, the cops doubled down and began deploying tear gas to disperse crowds. Police showed up in riot gear and shot rubber bullets at unarmed crowds. Armoured forces waded into crowds and cracked heads with billy clubs and full-force takedowns.

"Cops blamed for street artist's fatal fall"

"Police actions led to ladder fall"

"Police lied, rules High Court"

In the days ahead, disturbing videos from around the UK of what was being called police ultraviolence continued to circulate with alarming regularity.

The unrest in the London streets intensified. Peaceful protests turned into ugly confrontations when armoured police officers waded into the crowds and began knocking people down or pushing them off their feet. And when the crowds retaliated by smashing windows and looting stores, they were met with billy clubs and rubber bullets. Crudely written—and often, just plain crude—graffiti tags and slogans were written across storefronts in several boroughs, with Shoreditch especially hard hit.

As the unrest grew, so did the police presence in the streets, which resulted in even more media coverage. Videos circulated of police clubbing protesters and throwing them into unmarked vans. Cops cornered crowds and then fired tear gas canisters at them. Officers leaned out of police van windows to fire tear gas at groups of kids. It was especially hard to argue with allegations that the police were using unnecessary force, when the video evidence was edited to show only the parts of the story the agitators wanted to show.

The "spraycan thrower" still-frame image from Alec's video became a viral meme and a huge number of variants began to circulate on social media. The thrower hurled anything from a bouquet of flowers to a wad of money. He threw darts, nukes, paper airplanes, small children and animals, Brexit threats, an *Art for Dummies* book, and just about everything else. There were even some clever 'meta' references, where he threw recursively smaller versions of his own image, Warhol soup cans, or other famous art pieces by Fairey, Banksy, and others.

Other variants substituted different figures. Politicians threw away votes, human rights, oil deals, and whatever else the topic of the day might turn to. The editorial cartoonists had a field day.

A few days later the meme had evolved to a point where the spraycan was gone, the thrower was someone or something else (mash-up references to Star Wars, Star Trek, Disney or pop-culture celebrities were popular), and you wouldn't even know what was going on unless you knew about the *other* memes that were being meta-spoofed. Darth Vader was throwing a lightsaber to a Star Wars kid.

The Design Awards stirred the pot again a few weeks later when it was announced that the Dreamteam's design for the PAUL IS DEAD campaign poster was shortlisted for the Design of the Year award. Alec was credited as the creator of the image, which his lawyer subsequently disavowed. In a statement, Alec's lawyer was quoted as saying "there is no evidence to suggest that my client is in any way associated with the property or affairs of the unidentified party known as "TCO."

The original 'MISSING' wall-art idea reappeared as a widely distributed sticker series with a slightly modified "M SS NG" caption, although no one on the team could figure out who was responsible for the design, or the release. They wondered if the missing 'I' characters were a reference to the dreamteam's "be invisible" philosophy, but the question was never resolved.

On the day of the interment of the ashes, Johnnie wept as the funeral rites were read. Petra stood between Paul's parents and a couple of middle-aged people Len didn't know. Georgia and After Midnight stood next to Dal, who recorded the event for Alec.

After the funeral, Len wasn't much in the mood for socialising. A text from Danielle arrived. "I'm going back to Paris on Sunday," she said. "Are u coming over?"

"Sorry, not feeling too good today. Will call u soon," he replied.

He hopped on his motorbike and headed for home. When he got there, he noticed a silver and blue limousine parked outside his house. After locking the motorbike, he walked over to the car. The rear window rolled down. "Get in," said the woman Len had only seen from a distance before.

"I don't believe we've met," said Len, as politely as his racing mind would allow.

"My friends call me Duckie," said the woman. "I hope we can be friends."

* * *

New evidence came to light that while Alec was in jail, new artworks attributed to the anonymous TCO appeared around town.

There was also one notable disappearance. The RE-THINK mural was cut out of the wall and spirited away by an unknown party. Len and Petra went back and wrote MISSING below the now-empty hole in the wall, as Paul had originally envisioned.

Len called Danielle several times that week, but she never picked up or returned the calls.

The cellphone that captured the incriminating video was shown to be associated with a service plan registered to TCO, casting doubt that Alec was present.

The newspapers reported that Alec was *not* the mysterious and elusive artist. The appeals court held that there was reasonable doubt that Alec had been the anonymous ringleader. This led to many of the charges against him being dropped, including the most serious felony charge of "conspiracy."

The successful legal appeal saw the term of the sentence reduced from 36 months to nine.

* * *

A patch of green grass lay between a modest but well-kept brownstone house, and beyond it, a rough garden of wild poppies surrounded a small dark-brown wooden garden shed. As the tall poppies swayed almost imperceptibly in the gentle breeze, one of the pane-glass windows was pushed open. In her garden-shed studio, Petra stood in the light from the window and looked at the floating dust motes, now moved by the air currents coming in through the open window. She looked again. No, they were moving *out* of their sleepy world into the open air.

She picked up a black box and put it down on the floor. She opened the box of ashes and half-filled an empty can, then tipped the can and stirred the ashes into a wide-mouthed glass container of grey paint. Behind her stood a large canvas, primed and stretched and, around it, a variety of brushes and other bottles of brightly coloured paint. She stirred the ash into the paint for a moment and then, with a large brush, began blocking in a tall gray rectangle on the canvas.

Behind her, and all around her, other canvases and sketches stood in various states of completion. Many were based on sketches from Paul's piece book.

Two weeks later, Georgia climbed the small step-stool and adjusted the lights in the presentation room of the Smash Gallery. The picture on the wall was Petra's completed "Stellengard" painting. And there, inside the shadows of the grey alcove, was the face of Paul, looking fragile and brave.

* * *

Two Years Later

One sunny Monday morning in May, Georgia looked up and saw Len standing outside the front window of her new gallery on Hoxton Street. She opened the front door. "Well, what a nice surprise," she said. "This is your first time here, isn't it?"

Len nodded "It sure is."

"Do come in. I'll give you the grand tour."

"Sure, if it's not too much trouble." "None at all. That's the neon section over on that side—After Midnight manages that section—and this is our fine art section here. You probably recognize this one."

It was his Moloko poster, now priced at £950. "They've gone up in value," said Georgia. "Exciting, eh?"

"I guess," said Len.

"Hey," said Georgia, "Any idea whatever became of that woman that we chased around—what was her name?"

"Duckie, AKA the Duchess," said Len. "Yeah, I know a little about her. She approached me privately at one point and offered me the kind of deal that Alec used to offer us, you know, where we'd produce pieces and sell them outright, along with their copyrights. Apparently, she was Alec's hidden partner in that whole deal. She wanted me to enlist you and the rest of the team again, the way we used to operate, where she would pay Alec in secret, and he would pay us, and we'd theoretically never know she's in the picture."

"Yeah, those were shitty deals. I'm so glad you guys aren't doing that stuff anymore."

"Me too. But I can understand why Alec did it, I guess."

"'Cause he was keeping most of the money. No big surprise there."

"So, what happened?"

"It all went to hell rather quickly," Len said. We'd rented this studio space—just a little hole in the wall—where we could produce posters and silk-screen prints and stencils and things like that. And a little corner where we'd keep our tarps and paints and stuff for the dreamteam jobs, you know? So that was all good. You know, costs were low and Alec had all these supposed customers—which turned out to be his *patron's* customers—and then he got thrown in jail and it all went belly-up."

"Suddenly the money supply dried up. I'd already moved out of my place into my own flat, so I was scrambling around for a few months trying to make ends meet. I had just made a down payment on a motorbike, so that was especially annoying when it looked like I was going to lose that. Anyway, I had to give up the flat. Believe it or not, I was sleeping on the floor in the back of the workshop for about five months, just trying to make enough money to keep going. It was rough. But, you know, I had some good customers, made a couple of good deals with them and carried on. Like they say: keep calm and carry on."

Georgia knew what Len must have been going through. She'd been there, too. "Wow. But you pulled through."

"Yeah. You remember Dal, I'm sure?"

"Of course."

"Well, Dal and I followed this woman—Duckie—on a couple of occasions. He's pretty funny with that invisibility trip of his, but he's really good at not being seen, so I guess it's working for him. We followed her all over the place and found out about all these deals she had going, and messed with her a bit."

"Do you still see Dal much?"

"No, not really."

"He's a silent partner in this gallery, you know. In fact, he's supposed to be here for the gala opening this Friday night. You're coming to that, I hope?"

"I wouldn't miss it," said Len. "Oh yeah, I was telling you about Duckie..."

"The last time I heard about her, she was caught selling fake copies of Keith Haring prints, saying they are signed by the original artist, but they're just knock-offs with fake signatures, you know? All sorts of stuff, supposedly authentic street art, but completely fake. She used to be known as the Duchess, apparently. But she was never an actual duchess. Really pathetic. Just another sad old hustler."

"Well," said Georgia, "she and Bill sound like a perfect pair."

Twelve

Rule 42

Ring ... Ring ...

In a dark, cramped room, an unshaven figure wearing a white sleeveless undershirt and a pair of jeans stood up and approached the Venetian blinds covering the room's only window, his hair messy and long. He poked a pair of fingers through the slats of the blinds and peered through the gap, squinting as he picked up the phone. "Hello?"

"What time are you going down to that grand opening thingie at the new Smash Gallery tonight?" Len asked.

"I don't think I'm going to go at all, actually," replied Alec.

"Come on man, you should definitely go. It's quite a big deal, I hear. Champagne, hors' d'oeuvres, you know, the whole bit. And we've got to support our friends, right? The whole dreamteam crew is going to be there, I hear. I could give you a ride if you like."

"Nah, I don't think so," said Alec. "But thanks for the offer. I've got to go. Thanks for calling. Bye." Alec hung up the phone and butted out a cigarette in an overflowing ashtray on his filthy coffee table. He picked up a lighter, then ran his fingers through the long bangs hanging over his face and tucked the hair behind his right ear as he raised a glass pipe to his lips.

* * *

Georgia heard a rap on the front door. She looked at her watch. Ten to seven. As she approached, she could see Len peering through the front window. He saw her coming and smiled through the glass as she unlocked the door. Instead of the business attire she usually wore, Georgia was dressed in an absolutely spectacular 1920s cocktail dress, all done up in sequins in an Art Deco motif, with a flapper hairstyle and jewelry to match. She looked like a character right out of *The Great Gatsby*.

"Well, look at *you*," she said, admiring his flamboyant *Art Nouveau*–themed vest.

"Me? *You* look amazing," he countered. "That is a great look on you."

The dress was particularly striking in proximity of any of the neon sculptures, of course, and Georgia was clearly enjoying the attention she drew. "You're the first one here," she said as he took off his jacket.

"I hate to miss out on the hors d'oeuvres," he teased her with a wink.

"Turn around, will you?" she asked him and he did so to show off the pattern on the back of the vest. She hadn't seen him this smartly dressed before. Quite a change.

"I thought maybe I could help with a few things," he said as he hung up his jacket.

"Why, thank you," she replied. "Do you think you could tape this to the glass near the front door? Facing out, of course." She handed him a small sign and a tape dispenser.

Len examined the sign. "*Closed for a private party,*" it said in Garamond italics. "Of course." He briefly considered affixing it upside-down. Or with a photocopier, he could turn it into petals of a flower. Or perhaps some coloured felt pens... Nah. He taped it up.

Georgia nodded to him her approval when she unlocked the door at seven o'clock sharp. Within the hour, Dal, Johnnie, and Petra all arrived, scrubbed up well and immaculately dressed.

After Midnight was *arguably* well-dressed too, in a pair of skinny-leg black pants and a slightly shiny maroon-coloured paisley suit jacket that, despite being something that would look ridiculously flamboyant at any other time, managed to look relatively understated compared to Georgia's eye-catching attire. He coupled his paisley style with a pair of slightly over-the-top vintage loafers.

Georgia sidled up to him and whispered, "Where's your bowtie?" "It's in my pocket," he replied, as if the bow tie would somehow have made it all too much.

"I brought some gifts," Len said as he opened his backpack. He pulled out a handful of dark gray hoodies, emblazoned with the dreamteam ambigram logo. "I've got eight of them here, so there should be enough for everybody."

"Aw, it's great," said Dal. "I can look *down* at it, or you shrimps can look *up* at it."

Georgia laughed. "This will look *terrible* with what I'm wearing tonight. But I'm putting it on anyway!"

"There's one here for you too, Mister Midnight, sir."

He winked. "Oh please, call me After." He held it up and admired it. "Nice lettering. So you guys are the dream team, eh?"

"Yep. And now so are you."

The dream team stood in a semicircle and raised their glasses to Georgia and After Midnight.

"So, is it 'New Smash' or '*The* New Smash'?" asked Petra.

Georgia smiled. "I was wondering that until the sign went up out front," she said, with a knowing look at After Midnight. "Apparently it's 'New Smash Gallery'."

"Sounds all right, doesn't it?" asked After Midnight, plucking an appetiser from a passing plate.

"Oh yeah, of course. And I think it looks fabulous, like a sign from the golden age of neon. It should have *always* been done up in neon."

"But what'll you call it when it's not *new* anymore?" asked Dal.

"We'll have to move again, I guess. Maybe to Old Street, eh?" Georgia winked at him. "So, what have you been up to, Dal?"

"You know that TV advert for the High Street tours? The one with that theme song, '*High Street Hi*'?"

"Yeah, I think I do know that. That jingle is *so* catchy."

"I produced that. That jingle's actually based on an old

Deaf School song called '*Hi Jo Hi*.' My dad helped me get the reproduction rights and all the legal stuff done and we licensed it and got the band to redo the track for the spot."

"No kidding? That sounds like fun."

"Yeah, it's done pretty well. Great bunch, they are. We won a London Tourism Award for that one."

"Wow, congrats! So, do you think Alec will be here tonight?"

"No, I don't think so," Dal said, shaking his head.

"I talked to him earlier and offered him a ride over here," said Len. "He didn't sound too good. I think it's been rough for him since he got out, y' know?"

"Is he out of prison? I thought he was in for something like three years?"

"No, there was an appeal and he only had to serve nine months."

"Still, jeez, nine months. Poor guy."

"I never heard how you guys managed to figure out where he lived," said Johnnie.

Len explained to the crew what happened.

"When I was in the van, I found the vehicle registration in the glove compartment and made a note of what we thought was Alec's address. But, as we discovered, it was actually Dal's address. It was a bit sneaky, I know. Sorry about that, Dal."

"S'alright. I'm pretty snaky sometimes myself. Oh, you said *sneaky*? Nevermind," he winked.

"The good news there is that Dal lives in a swanky house in a very posh neighbourhood, and he seems to have a very nice mum, so we strongly approve of that. Nevertheless, that whole excursion *was* a bit of a wild goose chase. So we tried again a few days later. We tried following Dal's car, assuming that he would be heading back to Alec's house to drop him off. Long story short: that was *also* a wild goose chase. Although we did learn that Danielle lives on a nice houseboat. Which we also approve of."

Petra waved her hand. "I was along for the ride on that effort. At that point, I gave up."

"And so did I," added Georgia. She raised her glass and tipped it toward Len. "But Len can be—oh, what's a kind word for it?—*tenacious.*"

"Ah, you are too kind," said Len, who then proceeded to provide a truncated version of the events on the night he ended up in the water. "So, I finally managed to follow Alec back to his house on foot and that's how I managed to convince Georgia to *please* give me one more chance to redeem myself, by proving to her that I had found it."

Georgia smiled and said: "And what do you know? As we sat there in my car the next morning waiting for Alec to come out, he fell asleep just *minutes* before Alec stepped out of his house. He would have missed it entirely if not for me! But my hat's off to you, Len. You never gave up and you would have really impressed me if you hadn't fallen asleep *at the worst possible time.*"

"Hey come on, that was the punchline of the story I was going to tell about *you.*"

Johnnie snorted.

"Eh, I probably should have taken Georgia's advice early

on. She wanted to just follow Dal from his place to Alec's on Tuesday before our meeting."

Dal shook his head. "Nah, that wouldn't have worked. We were always very snaky." I used to warn him against unwise pickups and dropoffs like that."

Petra looked impressed. "Oh, so you were the brains of the organisation all along. Nicely done."

"So Len," said Johnnie. "Was there ever a moment when you thought of giving up this rather foolish and clearly obsessive quest of yours?"

"Well," Len admitted, "I did have one last plan I was working on. Once we learned about the woman known as The Duchess and discovered where she lived, my obsessive curiosity got the best of me *again* and I began wondering what she did and how she kind of fit into this whole picture, you know?

"I don't know anything about this woman? Who is she?" Petra asked Johnnie, confused. He shrugged. "Who is this Duchess?"

"Well, for starters, we're pretty sure she's not a real Duchess," said Len. "She pulled up in this very fancy old limousine outside Alec's house. I was trying to figure out what Alec did when he was not with us and that's when I saw him getting into this really fancy car with an older woman. And then she approached me at Paul's interment and was acting rather suspicious, shall we say?"

"Do tell," said Georgia. "I've never heard this part before."

"I didn't want to pester Georgia for a ride again..."

"Correct thinking," she interjected.

"…but as she'd already been kicked off of the team, I decided to ask Dal, who, as we've all discovered, is like some super-powered invisible ninja when he decides he wants to be."

Dal smiled and said: "What can I say? I've been practicing."

"Anyway, Dal and I figured she might be the one payin' Alec's bills, so we followed her. We drove around listening to his *High Street Hi* jingle—which pretty much became our theme song—and followed her *everywhere* for a couple of days, eh Dal?"

"And the super weird thing about this woman," added Georgia, "is the fact that her chauffeur is my ex-husband. In fact, I *think* she's probably the one he was having his affair with."

"What?" exclaimed After Midnight. "You mean *Bill* is her chauffeur—as in Bill that used to work at the old gallery?"

Georgia nodded and added: "Yep. Bill, as in my cheating ex-husband. I know what her perfume smells like and I've never even met her."

Len looked at After Midnight, worried that the conversation was veering into dark territory.

"I realised I'd smelled that perfume before," added Georgia. "But I couldn't quite figure out the connection. So I asked Bill. He kept changing his story. She was a business associate of his, he said at first. When I asked him what kind of business, he got all defensive and said she was a patron. Then she was just a friend. I realised they were having an affair. I asked him point-blank and he denied it to my face at the time, but I was right."

"That sucks."

"Not at all. I'm glad I found out."

"Anyway," Len continued, "Dal and I followed her around a bit, without being seen. Which Dal is extremely good at, by the way. So we think we know where she lives and we've managed to look up her name, based on the address. Her name, as far as we can tell, is Leisel Berk."

Johnnie raised his glass. "Yeah, Dallas!"

"Holy crap, look who's here."

Alec stood at the front door, his hair and jeans ragged.

Everyone fell quiet as he approached with a look of mild trepidation on his face.

"So glad you made it," said Georgia, giving him a welcoming hug. "Thank you. It means a lot to me."

"We were just talking about that night I went looking for you at your patron's house."

Alec frowned. "You weren't looking for me. You were looking for her, weren't you?"

"Not really. I just followed you."

And I followed them. I mean *her*," added Dal.

"I've been thinking about that night a lot," Alec said.

"Of course," agreed Len. "We all have."

"I think she might have been the one who tipped off the police. Perhaps to get back at me for disobeying a directive. So I think I was the liability that night when Paul fell."

Everyone went quiet for a moment.

Finally, Len said: "Hey, we're thinking of doing a little after-hours painting. Are you still up for that sort of thing?"

Alec shook his head. "Listen guys, the terms of my probation are quite strict. I'm essentially forbidden from engaging in any street art–related activities. I considered taking a more hands-off approach to managing the group but I think it will be better for the team if I bow out and let someone else take over. You guys can hire a manager if you want or you can elect one of you to lead—it's up to you. My dad has offered me a job at the Old Stag's Head, so if you want, I can keep the dreamteam table there for you and I'll see you if you drop by. I just wanted to see you guys and wish Georgia and After Midnight all the best."

"Thanks, you're a sweetheart," said Georgia affectionately. He'll be here later this afternoon to time to sign some pieces he's been working on—I'll be sure to let him know.

"So, I'm going to take off now. Go ahead and have a talk about this and let me know what you decide, okay? Whatever you choose will be fine with me. I trust you all."

The rest of the team weighed its options.

"Alec never betrayed us and I think it is only fair that we extend the same courtesy to him," observed Georgia. Len nodded and raised a finger. "I agree, but I don't give a hoot about whether we piss off his old patron or not. Ms. Berk approached me and, honestly, I don't want anything to do with her. I think we can create our own print-making business.

"We can—and should—own the rights ourselves. Maybe we can operate as kind of a collective, where we just help each other. I frankly don't care if we vote on things or just do them. I remember when Alec gave us that speech about great art doesn't come from a committee. I think I agree with that. It's more important to just *do* it. Street art is transitory anyway. To paraphrase old Will 'the Chill' Shakespeare: "The idea's the thing wherein we'll catch the conscience of the public. So, I say to you, let us be as masterless men—a guild united in purpose, yet unfettered by the interests of others."

The others nodded in approval.

He continued: "I would like to see a lot of the ideas that were never used come to some sort of fruition. You know, like those great ideas we came up with when we were first brainstorming concepts for the *Missing* project. Like, I always thought that a pair of machine gunners trying to shoot down a squadron of Mary Poppinses *but missing* could be quite an iconic image. And that idea of the royal guard with a missing hat eyeing a hat-shaped fuzzy little black dog as it walks by is an incredibly cute—not to mention uniquely British—image, as well. Just a bearskin hat with skinny little legs, you know?

"I think we should do all of them. When I think about the way we're all missing Paul, it just seems to be a perfect idea for us to be working on—you know, a whole series of pieces, all exploring the many meanings of the word."

"I love it," said Georgia. "A series of prints like that would definitely sell."

Petra, who was sitting next to Len, stood up. "Can I go next?" she said.

"Fine with me," said Johnnie. "I haven't got anything that can follow a big speech like Len's, anyway. Why don't we just go around the table in order?"

"As I'm sure all of you can manage, this has been a very difficult year for me. I can only speak for myself, but the concern I have about operating as a collective is the fact that

I feel like I'm more of an artist than a businessperson. I want a business manager to help me take care of those parts of the business that aren't really my forte, you know? I have nothing but respect for people who understand the finer points of tax law and corporate investment strategies, but that sure as hell isn't me. If Alec can't or won't take on that role again, I believe we—at least *I*—need to find someone else who can. That's all I wanted to say." She sat down. "Johnnie?"

Johnnie stood up. "I was thinking back to the time when Alec first interviewed me. I guess he picked all of us because we all had something valuable to offer. Anyway, I can't remember everything I said back then, but I remember that I was nervous and was just kind of bullshitting my way through the interview, pretending I knew what I was talking about. But I do remember one thing quite clearly that I said that day: I remember saying that we're a pretty good team. 'You should have all of us,' I said." His eyes welled up with tears. "I always thought that's why he chose us all. Because of what I said that day. I don't know if it's true," he said, wiping his eye. "I guess I should ask him about it some time. But I just wanted you all to know that's how I feel about us. We really do make a good team. And so that's valuable to me. That's all." He sat down.

"Right on, John," said Petra. "I guess you're next, Dal," she said.

"I don't really have too much to say," said Dal, "but I like this idea of doing the *Missing* ideas as a series of works. Some prints, some walls, some stickers, installations, or whatever— it's a good tribute to Paul, and it's a good tribute to Alec's leadership and everything that's happened since then, too. I think it would be a success. It's sort of like the core of our brand, like the thing that becomes the legend, you know?"

"Yeah, well said, mate," said Len.

* * *

Len sat on the couch in Alec's tiny flat. "Hi Bob, It's Len. Hey, I've got an idea that I think might interest you. You remember the idea you had to produce and print up your own posters? I was wondering if you might be interested in an exchange of services. I'll supply design services for Moloko and the Old Stag's Head in exchange for some space in your workshop. Yeah? Great. Sure, I'm open to that. Sounds great. Would you have any problem if I hired Alec to work with me? If he wants to, of course. You sure? Okay, perfect. When's good for you? Sure, I'll see you then."

Alec returned from the bathroom.

"I don't know about this, man," said Alec, sitting down.

"Think of it this way, Alec. As part of the deal, the company—I was thinking we might call it 'The Collective' or something like that—arranges to rent a portion of the workshop area, where the company hires me and you and the others to work. We produce and sell the work, and we keep the money. This will help us minimize our hard costs and it will help you repair the relationship with your dad, maybe?" Plus, we get access to the tools in your dad's workshop, so that saves us a bunch of money. And, I don't know, maybe we can even set up a little sales area like we used to have in the old design shop. You know, like the official dreamteam factory store."

"I dunno. The dreamteam was big news a couple of years ago, but it's not much of a brand any more, is it?"

"Or—what the hell! Why don't we just *steal* the TCO name and say *we're* the official store of TCO? Screw the Duchess!"

"Hah, you make it sound so easy," Alec said, rubbing his head nervously. "I don't think she'd stand for that. She's dangerous, I'm telling you. I don't want to get sued, and I don't want my dad to get into legal trouble, either."

"She'd have to reveal her identity herself to sue us."

"But we already *know* her identity, don't we?"

"Yes, but she doesn't know that."

"I don't know, man. Seems awfully risky."

"Look, if we set it up properly, she'd be suing a limited liability company, not us, personally. And frankly, I'd be willing to bet that most people would think that someone like you or I was more likely to be the secret identity of the notorious TCO, rather than some old woman."

"You've got a point there. It's a tantalising prospect, to be sure. We'd have to get approval from my father, though. It wouldn't be cool to get him into trouble or put his property at risk over this."

"Of course. Let's talk it over with your dad."

"Actually," said Len, "Let me have a chat with Dal about this...."

* * *

The elevator doors opened and Dal emerged with Len following on behind him. "It's this way," he said. "Number

402." Dal opened the door to the office and he motioned for Len to sit down. Dal spoke quietly to the receptionist. Len heard her greet Dal by name, so they clearly knew one another. She asked him how she should introduce his accomplice. Len couldn't quite make out his response, but her saw her smile.

Dal came and sat down in the chair next to Len. "He's just finishing up with a client," he said quietly.

The receptionist pressed a button on her phone, picked up a file folder and stood up. "Mister Barr will see you now," she said, motioning to an inner office door to the left of her desk. She led them into a room with a large wooden desk in front of set of bookshelves that covered nearly the whole wall. "Hullo Dad," said Dal. "This is my friend Len. Len's been teaching me about print production and, well, that's kind of what we are coming to you about."

"Pleased to meet you, sir," said Len, extending his right hand. Mr. Barr gave it a firm handshake. "Thanks for taking the time to meet with us," Len said with a smile.

"No problem," said Barr. "I understand you boys are looking for a little legal advice. What can I help you with?"

"Well, as Dallas mentioned, we've been working with a group of designers and artists on some projects that ran into some difficulties due to the actions of an associate of ours, whom I think you've heard of. His name is Alec."

"Yes, nasty business, that," said Barr. "I helped him get his sentence reduced."

Yes, that was fantastic. He's doing much better now. Anyway, the main concern we have at this point, is this woman whom Alec made a deal with. We're worried that this deal was—uh, what's the term? *Coercive.*"

"Yes, it's known as Contract Coercion, and it applies in cases where there is evidence of duress or undue influence in contract law. First of all, we need to establish whether there was, in fact, a binding contract. A basic binding contract must comprise four key elements: offer, acceptance, consideration and intent to create legal relations. In order to overturn such a contract, the court must find evidence that the contract was entered into as a result of undue pressure or undue influence. There are actually three different classes of undue influence, but the key point is whether the person who signed the contract received independent legal advice before signing. If they did, the courts will usually find that the contract is valid. If not, well, we might be able to make a case of it."

"I honestly don't know, said Len. "I do, however, know that that an offer was made to me that may have been similar, and based on the contract I saw, I would have been signing away all present and future rights, in all present and future media formats in perpetuity."

"I hope you did not sign that."

"I certainly did not."

"Have Alec contact me, will you? We'll need to get a sworn statement from him.

When I've spoken to him, we'll determine how to proceed. Thanks for coming in."

* * *

Three Months Later

The blue door at the back of the workshop opened and Len, wearing a stylish vest, stepped into the room. Accompanying him was a man in a business suit. "And this," said Len, "is the production area." He gestured to his right. "That's Petra, our design manager, at the design desk there."

To Len's left, light streamed out of the doorway of a smaller room as a figure wearing a respirator stepped out of the brightly lit room carrying one end of a painted Plexiglas fascia. "That's Dal, one of our producers, there, finishing up a final quality check on the light table," he explained.

Dal flashed him a thumbs-up signal as he passed.

As the figure carrying the other end of the plastic sheet drew nearer, Len said: "Ah, there he is. Allow me to introduce our business manager, Alec. He can answer all your questions about the lease, or anything else regarding the business side of things."

"I'll be right with you," said Alec. "Dal will get this last piece packaged up for you."

Alec returned a moment later. Hello again, Mr. Aldeen. A pleasure to see you again. You're right on schedule. Would you like to inspect the piece before we package it all up?

"Yes, that would be fine."

"It's right over here."

"Well, sir, I'll leave you in Alec's capable hands. I'll be in the shop until 4 pm if you have any additional questions for me."

Alec led Mr. Aldeen over to the table where the fascia lay face-down on a large sheet of brown wrapping paper. "That's the shipping dock there," Alec said, pointing to a wide doorway at the rear of the shop. "Just back your truck in there and we'll get all the pieces loaded up. You'll need two people to unload them safely at your destination, of course."

"Not a problem," said Mr. Aldeen. "You've been most helpful."

"It's been a pleasure to do business with you," said Alec, shaking his hand. "Thank you for choosing TCO."

A few minutes later, the truck's rear door was secured and Mr. Aldeen and his driver pulled out of the alley and onto the street past the front of the Moloko building.

At the front door of the Moloko, Georgia and Johnnie watched as the truck rolled by.

"Now that's the kind of customer I wish I had more of," said Georgia. "Paid in full upon delivery. Well done, Johnnie."

"To be fair," admitted Johnnie, "the lease was Alec's idea. I just made the sale."

"Attention: all staff please report to the main office. It's party time!"

Georgia and Johnnie crossed the floor of the Moloko, past several large and impressive installation pieces and opened the door to the stairwell that led up to the office in the mezzanine.

Inside, Alec popped the cork on a big bottle of champagne and filled glasses for everyone. "I want to thank the wonderful staff of TCO, makers of custom works of all shapes and sizes."

He handed a glass to Len. "For you, mister production manager. Thank you!

And to our fabulous designer, thank you." Petra smiled as he handed her a glass.

Alec then handed glasses to Georgia and Johnnie with a

smile. "And look at the well-deserved smiles on that sales team, ladies and gentlemen. Bravo!"

"And a special thanks to our man Dal, without whom probably none of this would have come about."

"My parents probably helped more than I did," confessed Dal. His parents had helped him set up a "licensed, bonded and insured" corporate entity that protected Bob Mack's interests, while allowing the dreamteam to operate cooperatively as an artistic collective, with each of them producing works to be released under the brand name TCO LLC.

"But yeah—yay for us!" He held his glass up. Cheers!"

As they all joined in the toast, Dal spoke again, "So much of this success, y'know," he said, is 'cause of you, Alec. You've been our business manager, managing the operation and planning the deliverables. Well, you and Len, I guess. Both of ya. Anyway, good on ya. Both."

"Here, here," said Petra, smiling at Len.

The next day, Len sent each of them a text calling for a special meeting at Bob Mack's pub on Tuesday at 7 p.m. to discuss what he characterised as "important legal matters."

By seven o'clock, everyone was there—and curious as to what the meeting was about. Len thanked everyone for attending and quickly turned the discussion over to Alec.

"As some of you know, Dal's mum and dad are in the legal business, and Dal and I have had a few meetings with them to try to work out some of the legal and copyright issues surrounding some of the works that the Duchess claims ownership of. Long story short: Dal's father believes that her claims to the copyrights are invalid and he is willing to work *pro bono* to get them returned to us.

There's relatively little risk to us personally, although there may be some liability to the TCO corporate entity. You see, the moment we take any action in the courts, the opposing party is essentially obligated to launch a countersuit in response.

So, we need to make sure we have all our ducks in a row.

Although the conditions imposed by Alec's parole limited his ability to participate, the plan they came up with was to produce deliberately infringing works based on their famous designs and sell what they were calling "uncertified originals." The goal, Len explained, was to force the Duchess to defend her original contract with Alec. By blatantly violating his contract with her, the onus was placed upon the claimant to show why the contract should be upheld. Dal's father believed that this would be sufficient to persuade the court that the original terms were unreasonable.

"It must be obvious from our subsequent works that they are by the original designers of the famous pieces that are the subject of the disputed copyright and ownership claims."

Predictably, the Duchess sued using a corporate shell. Dal's father handled the countersuit and helped the dreamteam in their legal battle and, using case law precedents from the music industry, it was determined that the prior art could be shown, the stencil was provably different, the paint and all other materials were different, the piece was identifiable as a unique piece, and the original artist's claim that coercion was involved in the signing of the original deal was upheld.

As a side effect of the legal wranglings, the Duchess' true identity was made public, information about some of her other shady dealings came to light, and Leisel lost the case. Ironically, although Alec's "TCO" signature on the limited-edition pieces was essentially bogus, it provided the proof of originality that won the case.

In the judge's decision, the original limited editions were rightfully paid for and remain the property of the defendant or subsequent purchasers or rights-holders of the works.

* * *

In a flat a few blocks away, a hand reached over a black leather-bound book with a Celtic knot pattern and pressed a rocker switch on an electrical cord hanging behind the side table. The neon noodles illuminating the flying spaghetti monster sculpture on the wall of the flat blinked into darkness. The front door closed and a moment later, Len emerged from the garage on a motorbike with a multi-coloured custom paint job.

Ten years after Alec's first meeting with the Duchess, the dream team was now responsible for more than ten million dollars of estimated TCO brand street art licensing and publishing revenue per year.

Alec shared the financial guidance, deal-making expertise, and art-world connections of his former patron with Len and the others. He and Len shared the management of the dreamteam, with Alec handling the business side of things, and Len keeping the production line running smoothly, with street art pieces and prints flowing onto the market and through the gallery channels. The team was now running as a collective, and the New Smash Gallery was just one of several galleries the team worked with. Auctions had taken over as the primary sales vehicle for the prints and originals that members of the team created, and sales of pieces by the dreamteam enjoyed unprecedented demand in the wake of all the news media coverage.

The Duchess had been completely cut out of the picture. Hers was the old world, where the paint had faded and the surfaces cracked. The workshop was now being advertised as the official "TCO Store" and the revitalised team prospered.

Alec was on the phone in the office. "Yeah, I'm doing all right, mum. Thanks for calling. Give my love to dad. I've got to go. Okay. I will. Bye-Bye."

Alec walked down the stairs and pulled open the big blue door to the workshop. He noticed Petra at her desk, examining a print for quality and there at the other end of the shop was Len, crouched down by the glass door. Curious, Alec moved closer for a better look. Len saw him approach. "Watch this," he said.

Len lightly rubbed his fingers over the delicate hairs of what he explained was called a gilder's tip and then held it over what looked like a booklet with golden pages. A sheet of gold leaf leapt off the page and, like magic, adhered itself to the surface of the gilder's tip. Len held the gilder's tip close to the glass and the gold leapt again, this time onto the glass door. "I've prepared the glass with a sticky clear glue called gilding size," he explained. "Come and take a look from out here," he said, opening the door and stepping outside to inspect his work. It was a "TCO" logo, elegantly rendered in silver and gold leaf.

"Wow," said Alec. "It's like a mirror."

"After this dries, I'll burnish the gold and then protect it with some varnish and a bit of protective paint."

"You're a wizard," said Alec with a smile.

"Looking good, guys," said Georgia, admiring the logo as she exited the building and jumped into the Cadillac waiting outside.

As After Midnight and Georgia drove down the A10, Georgia took a picture of a re-subvertised billboard reading "Suffering from Affluenza? Wash your hands more often—of responsibility."

"I think it is fucking hilarious that your silent partner—a real Mister Moneybags himself— is in part responsible for that."

"I know, I know!"

"Hey," said Georgia, "have you seen the new wall just down here, off Redchurch?"

"No! I forgot all about that. Where is it?"

"Just up ahead here, on the left. Slow down and I'll take a picture."

The caddy cruised slowly past a huge stenciled image of B-52s dropping Crayolas with brightly coloured splats on the ground below.

"I love it," said After Midnight.

The caddy pulled up in front of the New Smash Gallery. Georgia slid over and kissed him goodbye, then pushed open the big door of the car and climbed out. She paused for a second or two to look at the front door of the gallery, then swung it open and went inside, past the desk where Johnnie sits and the wall where *Stellengard* is marked not for sale.

The End

Other books in the Artworld series by Graeme Bennett

The Provenance of Stellengard

An artist is rumoured to have stolen her own work as a publicity stunt after a painting named Stellengard is stolen from a London gallery. A suspected art thief is arrested and Stellengard is recovered—or so it seems until another copy appears, and then a third. The provenance of the paintings and their bizarre backstories are put to the test.

Madder Lake

A red shoe and lipstick on a broken champagne glass are the only clues in the mysterious death of an artist who, as it turns out, has just painted his masterpiece. But the painting has disappeared. Many years later, the artist's adult son learns about the painting—and uncovers a secret that jeopardizes his future.

Other works by this author

BOOK ONE - HELIX

Scientists develop the technology to send matter forward—but only forward—in time. What they don't know is how their experiments are affecting the future world. The story focuses on the life-changing experiences of the first people to go forward, when there's no going back.

BOOK TWO - HAVEN

Corporatism catches up with a ruthless executive when an AI entity replaces him as CEO of a leading tech company and the world's most valuable intellectual property is stolen. It's the end of time at the last frontier.

BOOK THREE - HELIOS

A secret experiment in 1947 leads to contact with scientists and military strategists from the 25th century and a string of events in the U.S., China, Russia, and the Middle East that could lead to war.